31143011869477
J GN Descendants
Minami, Natsuki,
Descendents :
DISCARDED
Main

D0181545

ROTTEN TO THE CORE TRILOGY

MAL

JAY

CARLOS

EVIE

ADAPTED BY: JASON MUELL
ART BY: NATSUKI MINAMI

TOKYOPOP®

The story so far...

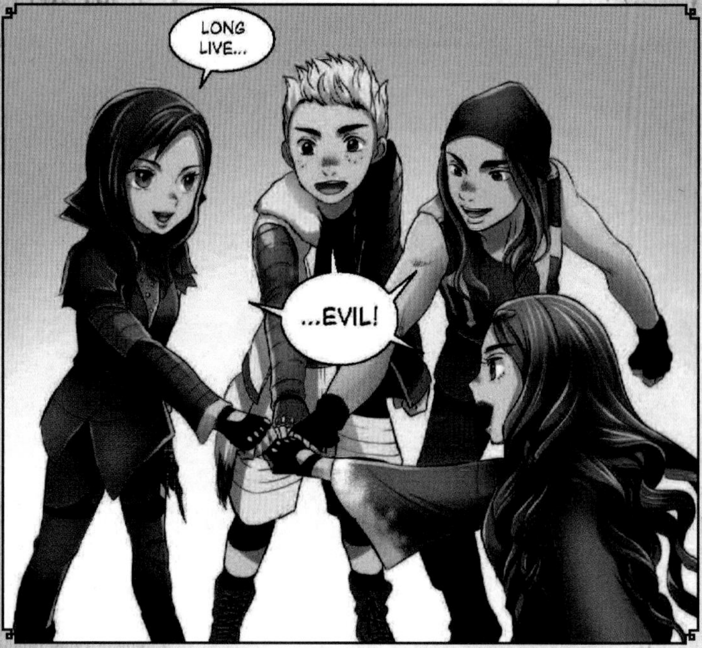
LONG LIVE...
...EVIL!

The VKs -- Mal, Evie, Jay and Carlos -- have been given a once-in-a-lifetime opportunity to escape the Isle of the Lost and attend Auradon Prep! Their first attempt to steal Fairy Godmother's wand has failed. But, rotten to the core and eager to please their evil parents, they're determined to release the villains from exile and let chaos reign over the people of Auradon.

Keep reading as Mal, Evie, Jay and Carlos continue their double lives at Auradon Prep...

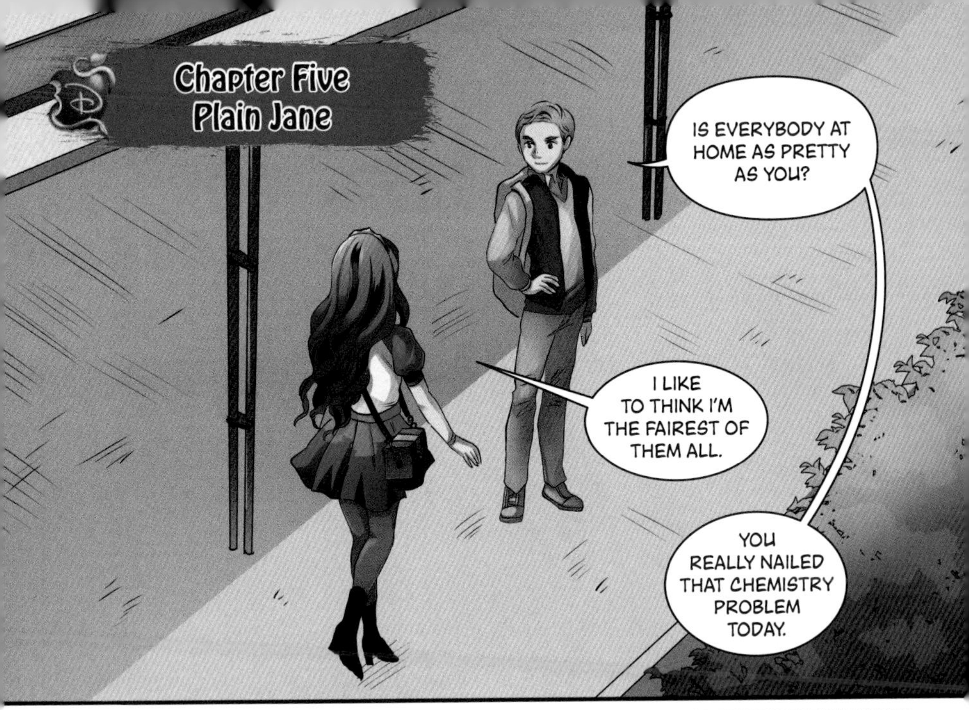
Chapter Five
Plain Jane
IS EVERYBODY AT HOME AS PRETTY AS YOU?
I LIKE TO THINK I'M THE FAIREST OF THEM ALL.
YOU REALLY NAILED THAT CHEMISTRY PROBLEM TODAY.
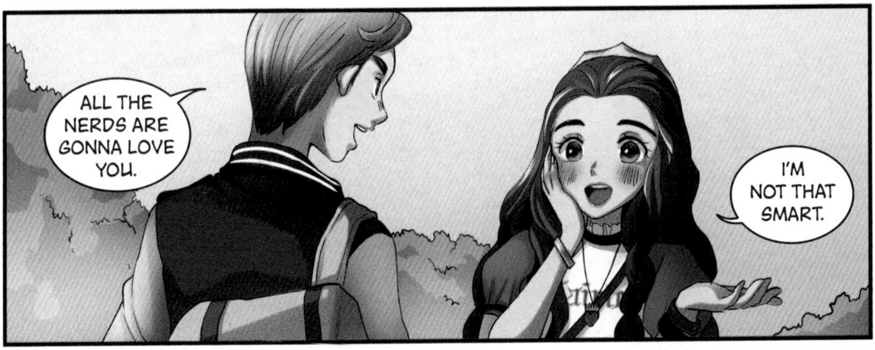
ALL THE NERDS ARE GONNA LOVE YOU.
I'M NOT THAT SMART.
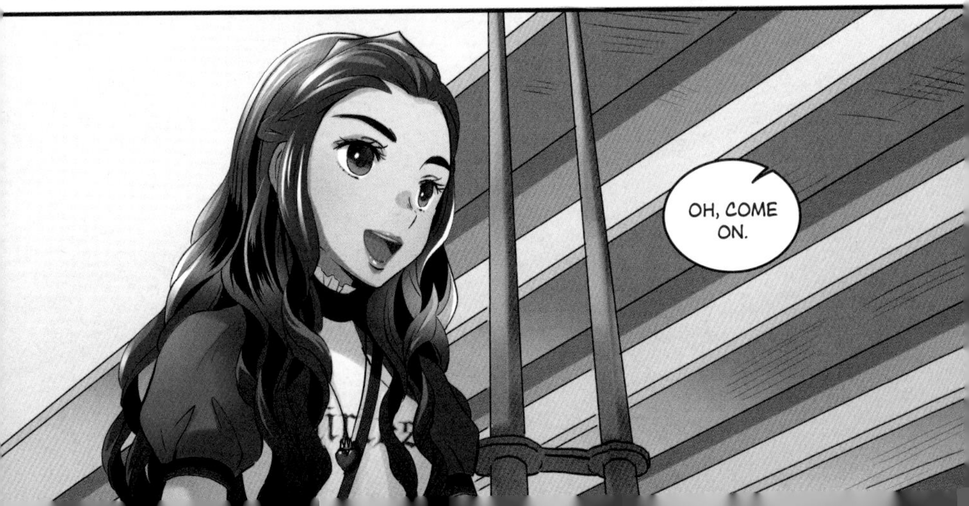
OH, COME ON.

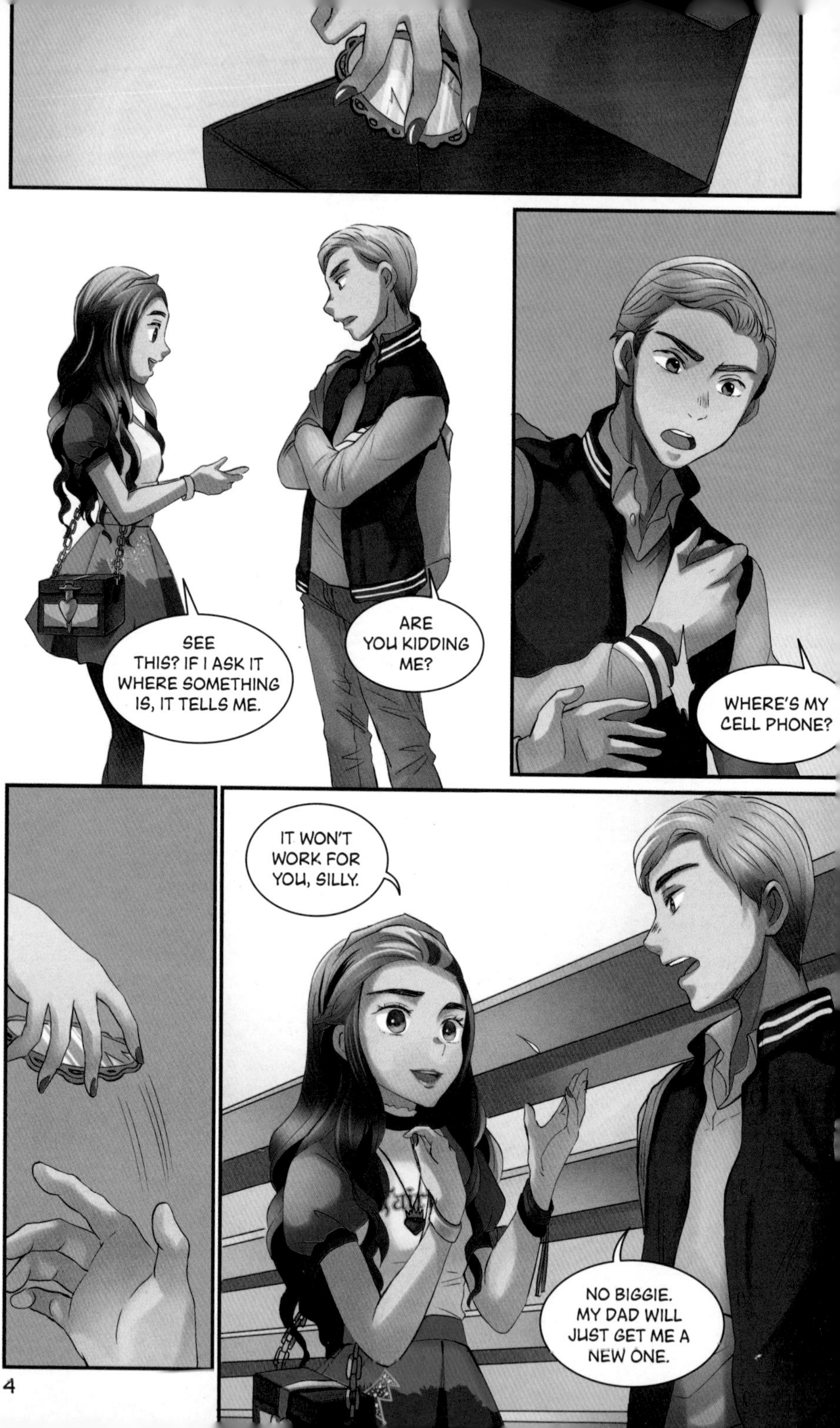
SEE THIS? IF I ASK IT WHERE SOMETHING IS, IT TELLS ME.
ARE YOU KIDDING ME?
WHERE'S MY CELL PHONE?
IT WON'T WORK FOR YOU, SILLY.
NO BIGGIE. MY DAD WILL JUST GET ME A NEW ONE.

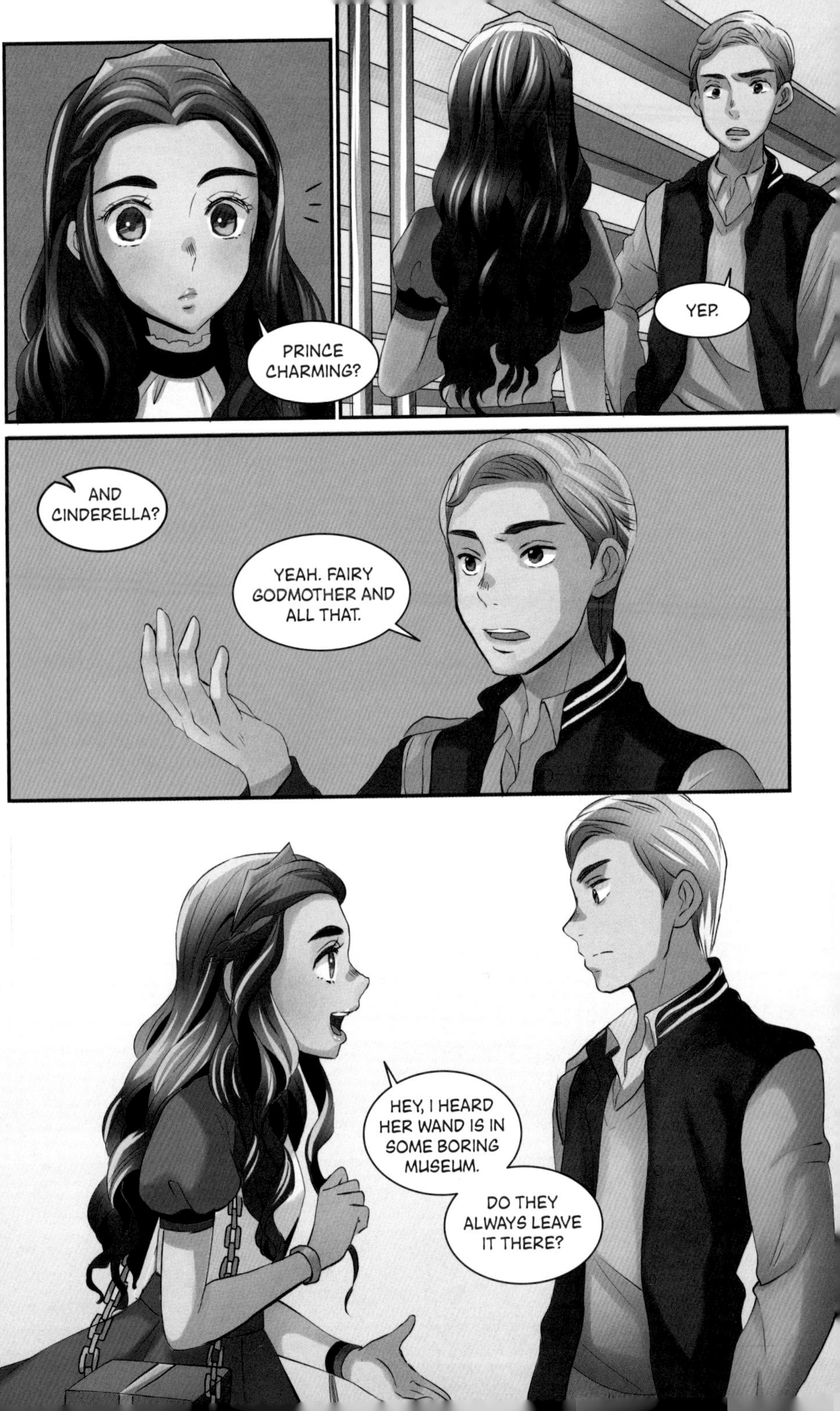
PRINCE CHARMING?
YEP.
AND CINDERELLA?
YEAH. FAIRY GODMOTHER AND ALL THAT.
HEY, I HEARD HER WAND IS IN SOME BORING MUSEUM.
DO THEY ALWAYS LEAVE IT THERE?

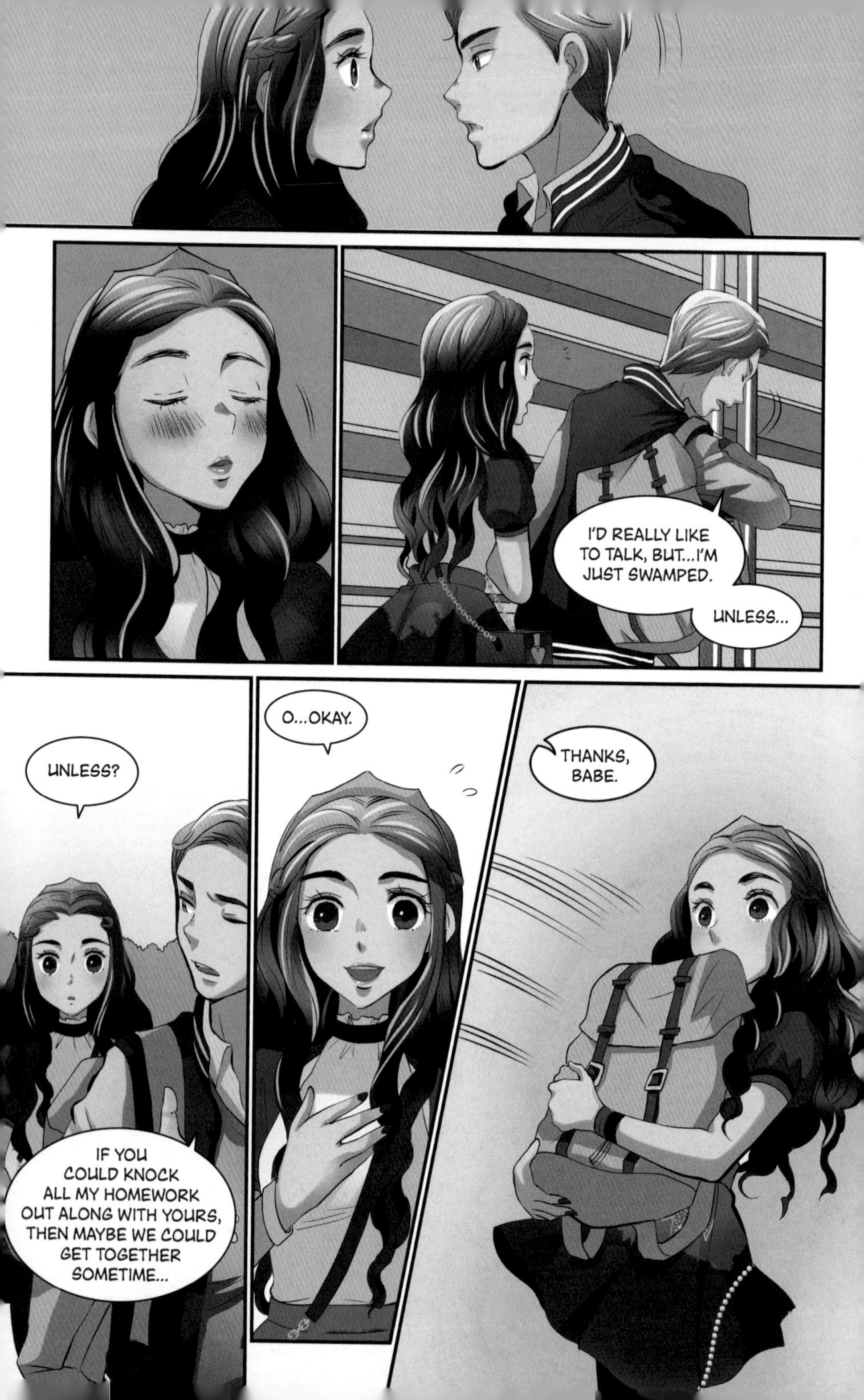
I'D REALLY LIKE TO TALK, BUT...I'M JUST SWAMPED.
UNLESS...
UNLESS?
IF YOU COULD KNOCK ALL MY HOMEWORK OUT ALONG WITH YOURS, THEN MAYBE WE COULD GET TOGETHER SOMETIME...
O...OKAY.
THANKS, BABE.

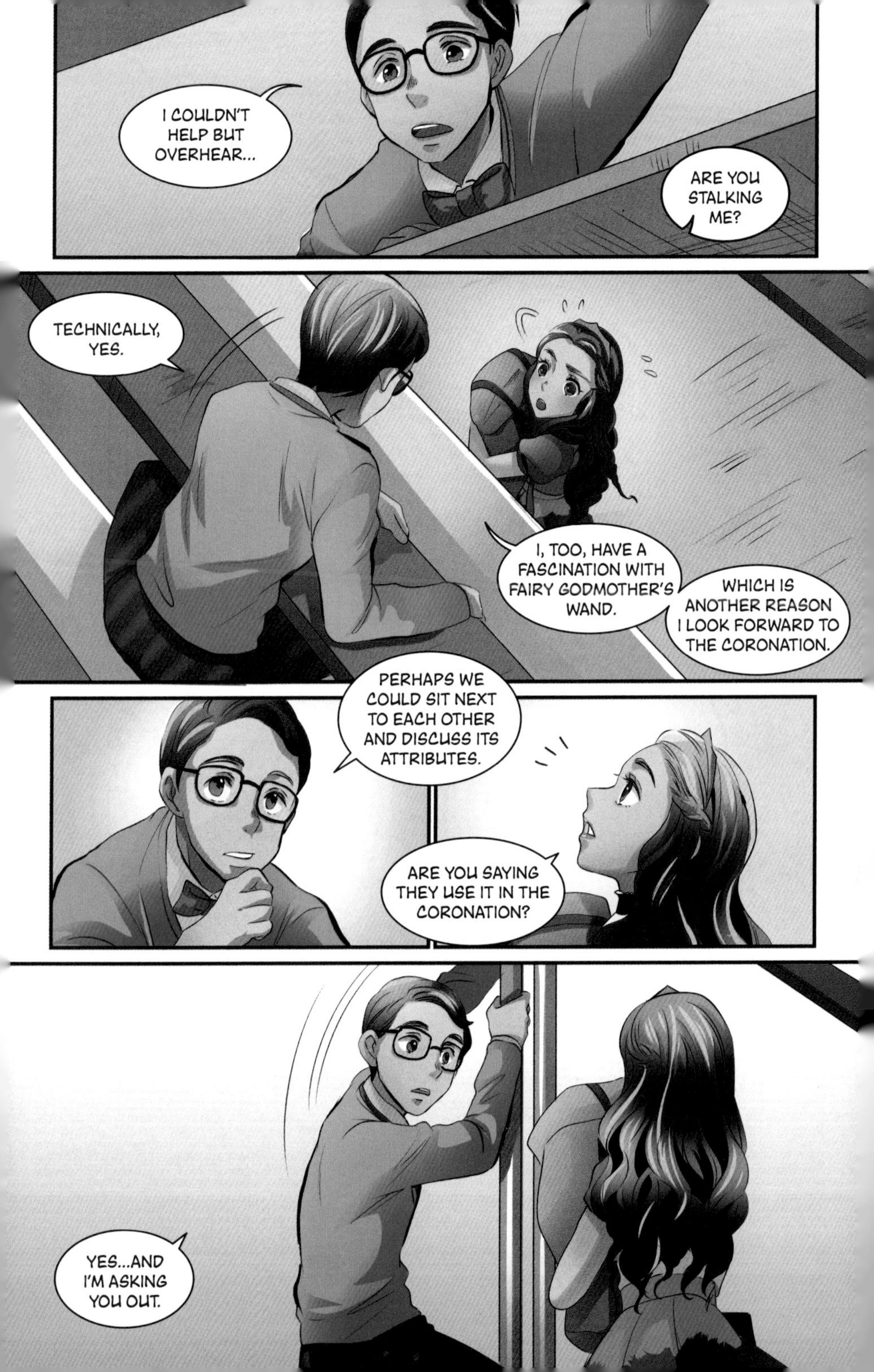
I COULDN'T HELP BUT OVERHEAR...
ARE YOU STALKING ME?
TECHNICALLY, YES.
I, TOO, HAVE A FASCINATION WITH FAIRY GODMOTHER'S WAND.
WHICH IS ANOTHER REASON I LOOK FORWARD TO THE CORONATION.
PERHAPS WE COULD SIT NEXT TO EACH OTHER AND DISCUSS ITS ATTRIBUTES.
ARE YOU SAYING THEY USE IT IN THE CORONATION?
YES...AND I'M ASKING YOU OUT.

MOM SAID "IF A BOY CAN'T SEE THE BEAUTY WITHIN, THEN HE'S NOT WORTH IT."

CAN YOU BELIEVE IT? WHAT WORLD DOES SHE LIVE IN??

AURADON?

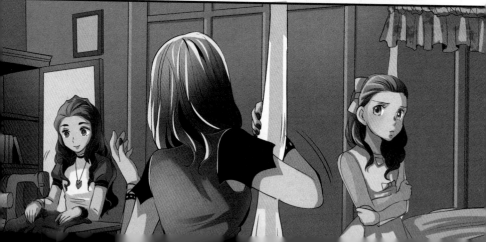

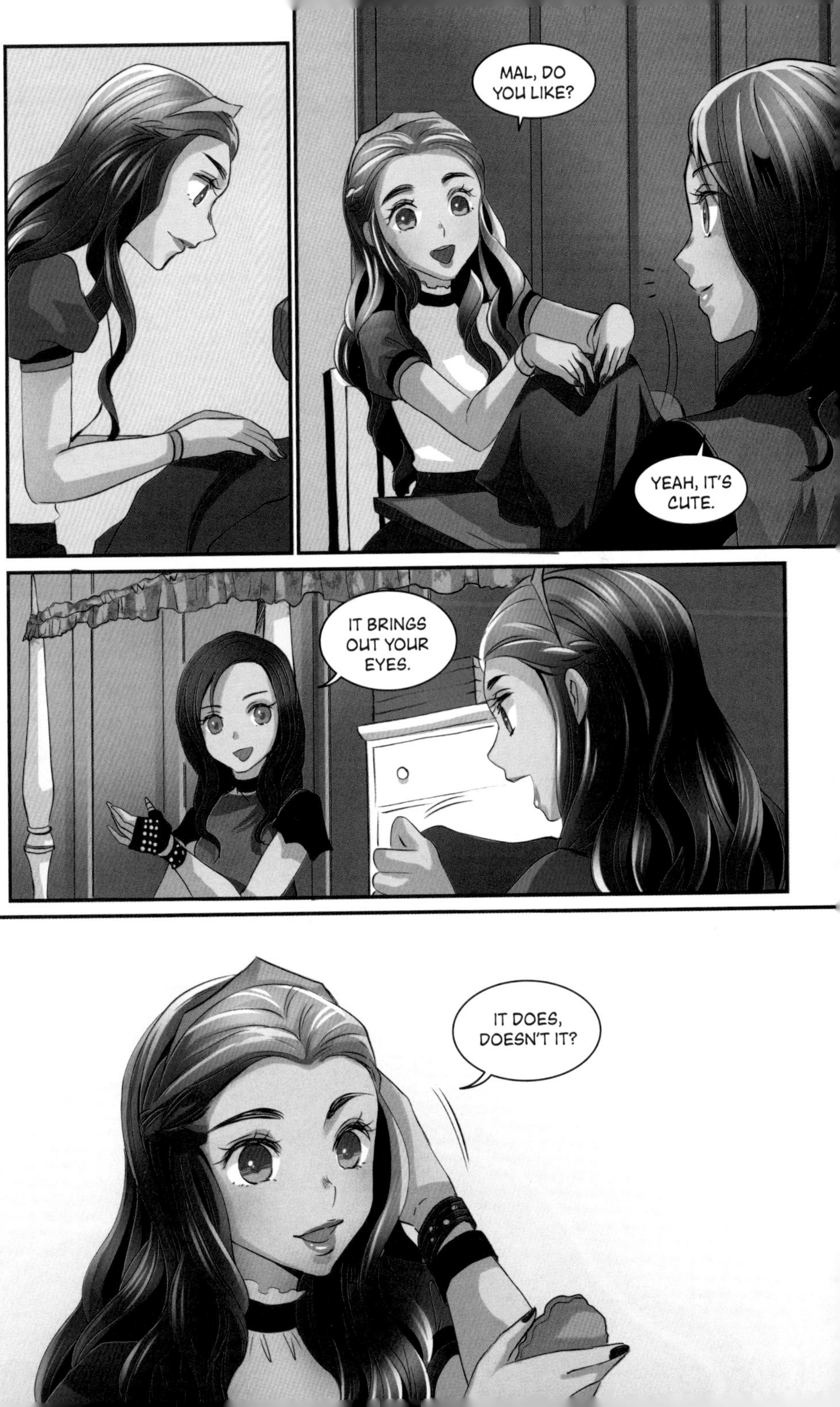
MAL, DO YOU LIKE?
YEAH, IT'S CUTE.
IT BRINGS OUT YOUR EYES.
IT DOES, DOESN'T IT?

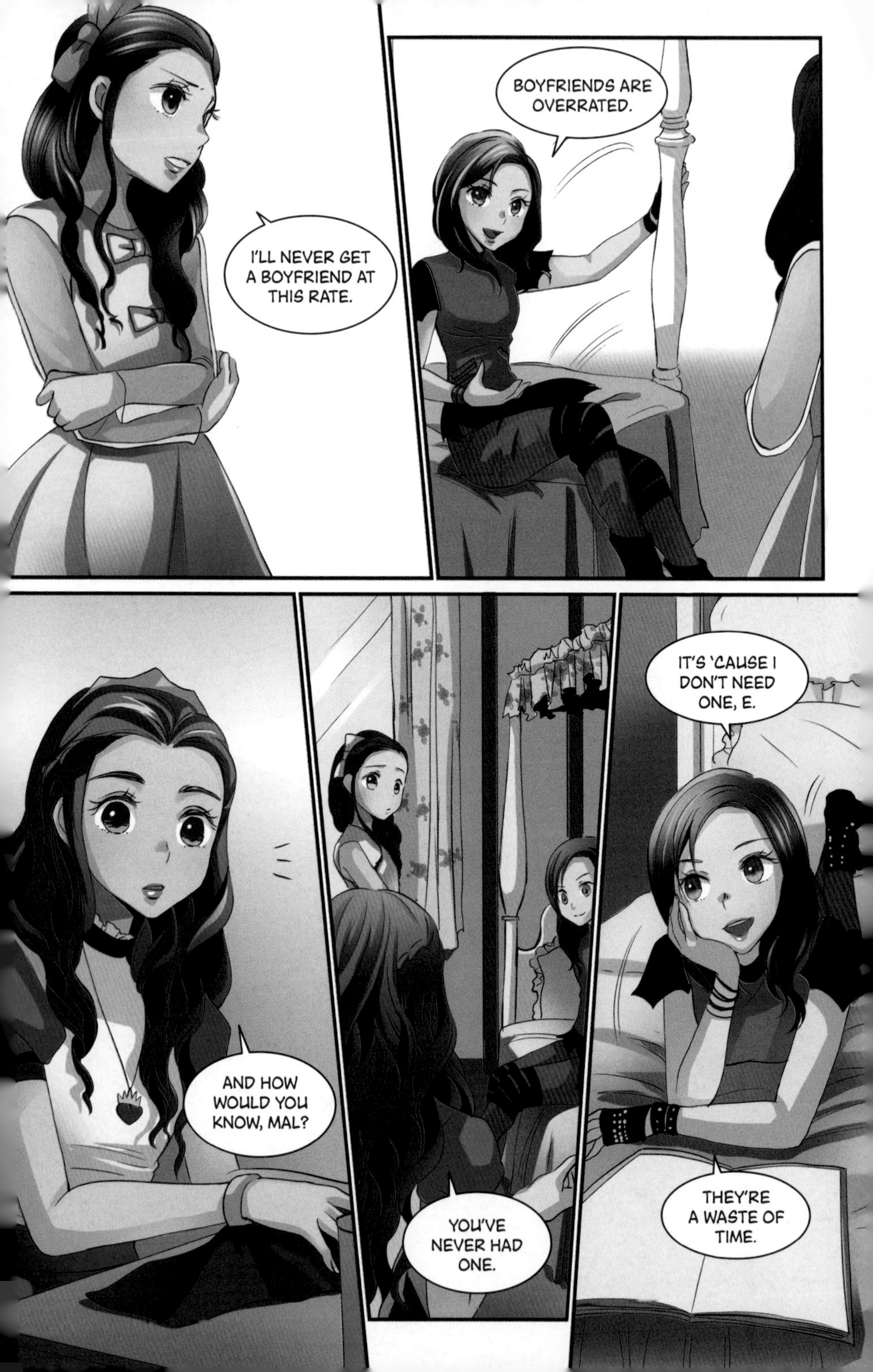
I'LL NEVER GET A BOYFRIEND AT THIS RATE.
BOYFRIENDS ARE OVERRATED.
AND HOW WOULD YOU KNOW, MAL?
YOU'VE NEVER HAD ONE.
IT'S 'CAUSE I DON'T NEED ONE, E.
THEY'RE A WASTE OF TIME.

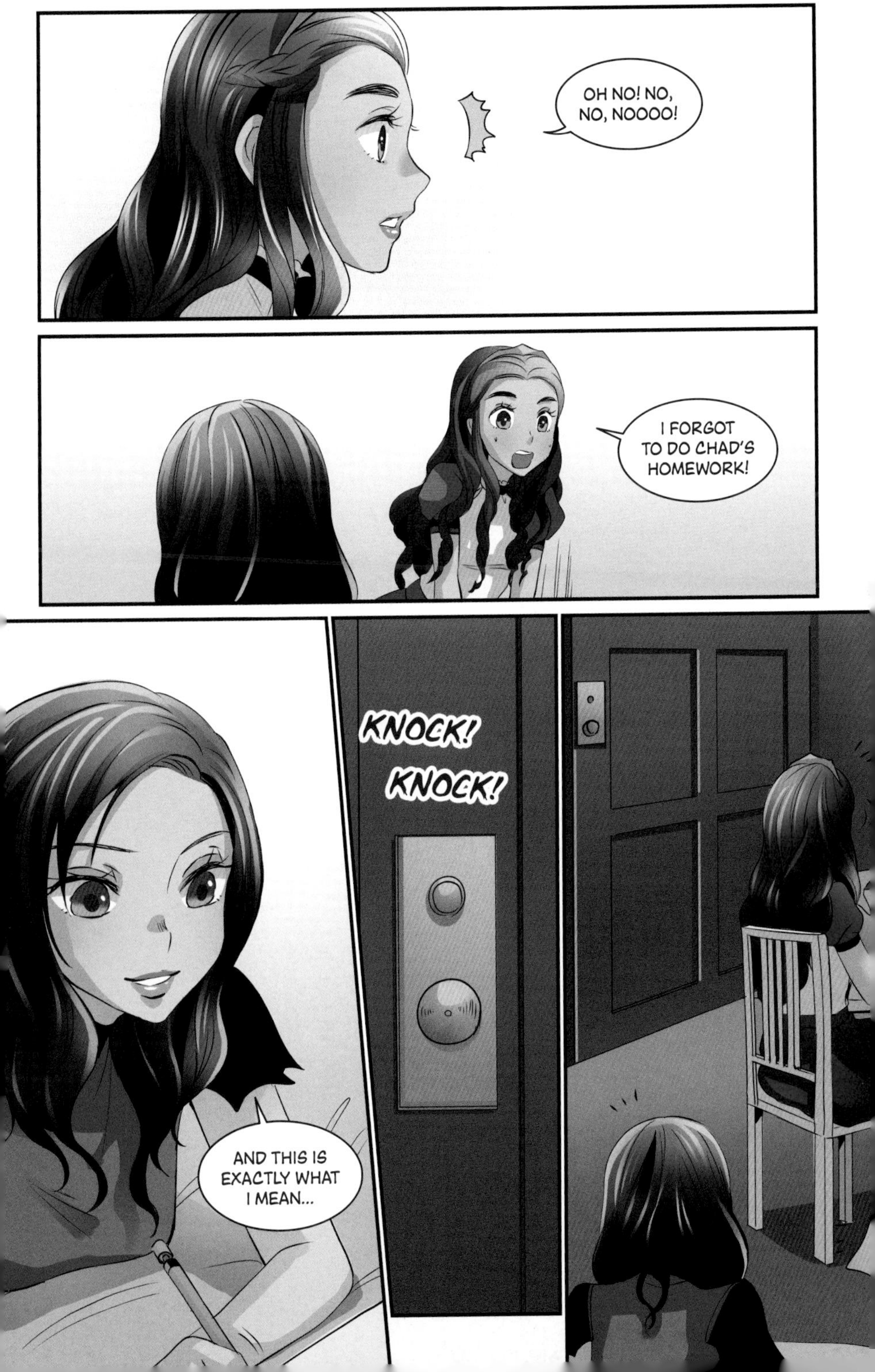
OH NO! NO, NO, NOOOO!
I FORGOT TO DO CHAD'S HOMEWORK!
AND THIS IS EXACTLY WHAT I MEAN...
KNOCK!
KNOCK!

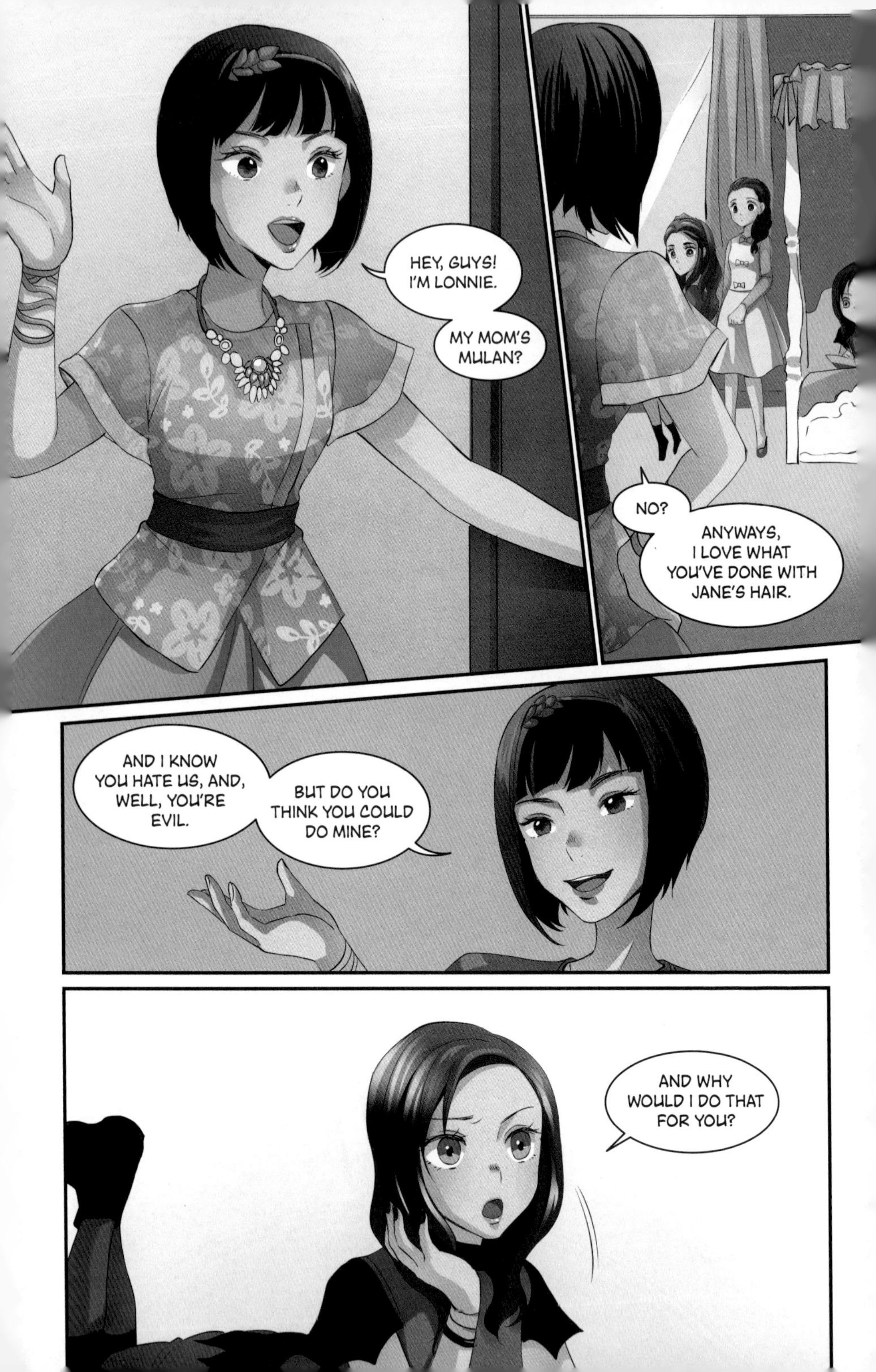
HEY, GUYS! I'M LONNIE.
MY MOM'S MULAN?
NO?
ANYWAYS, I LOVE WHAT YOU'VE DONE WITH JANE'S HAIR.
AND I KNOW YOU HATE US, AND, WELL, YOU'RE EVIL.
BUT DO YOU THINK YOU COULD DO MINE?
AND WHY WOULD I DO THAT FOR YOU?

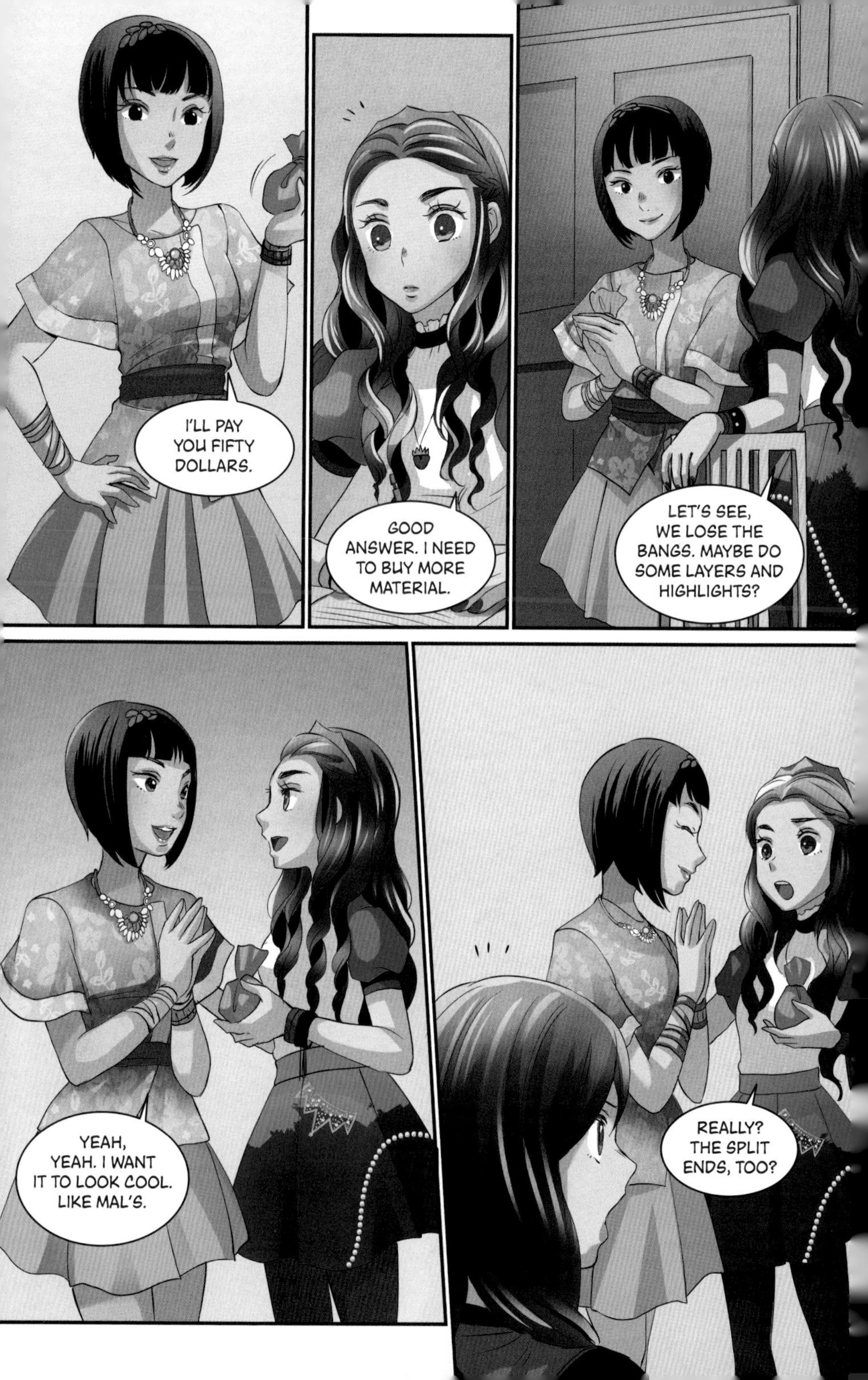
I'LL PAY YOU FIFTY DOLLARS.
GOOD ANSWER. I NEED TO BUY MORE MATERIAL.
LET'S SEE, WE LOSE THE BANGS. MAYBE DO SOME LAYERS AND HIGHLIGHTS?
YEAH, YEAH. I WANT IT TO LOOK COOL. LIKE MAL'S.
REALLY? THE SPLIT ENDS, TOO?

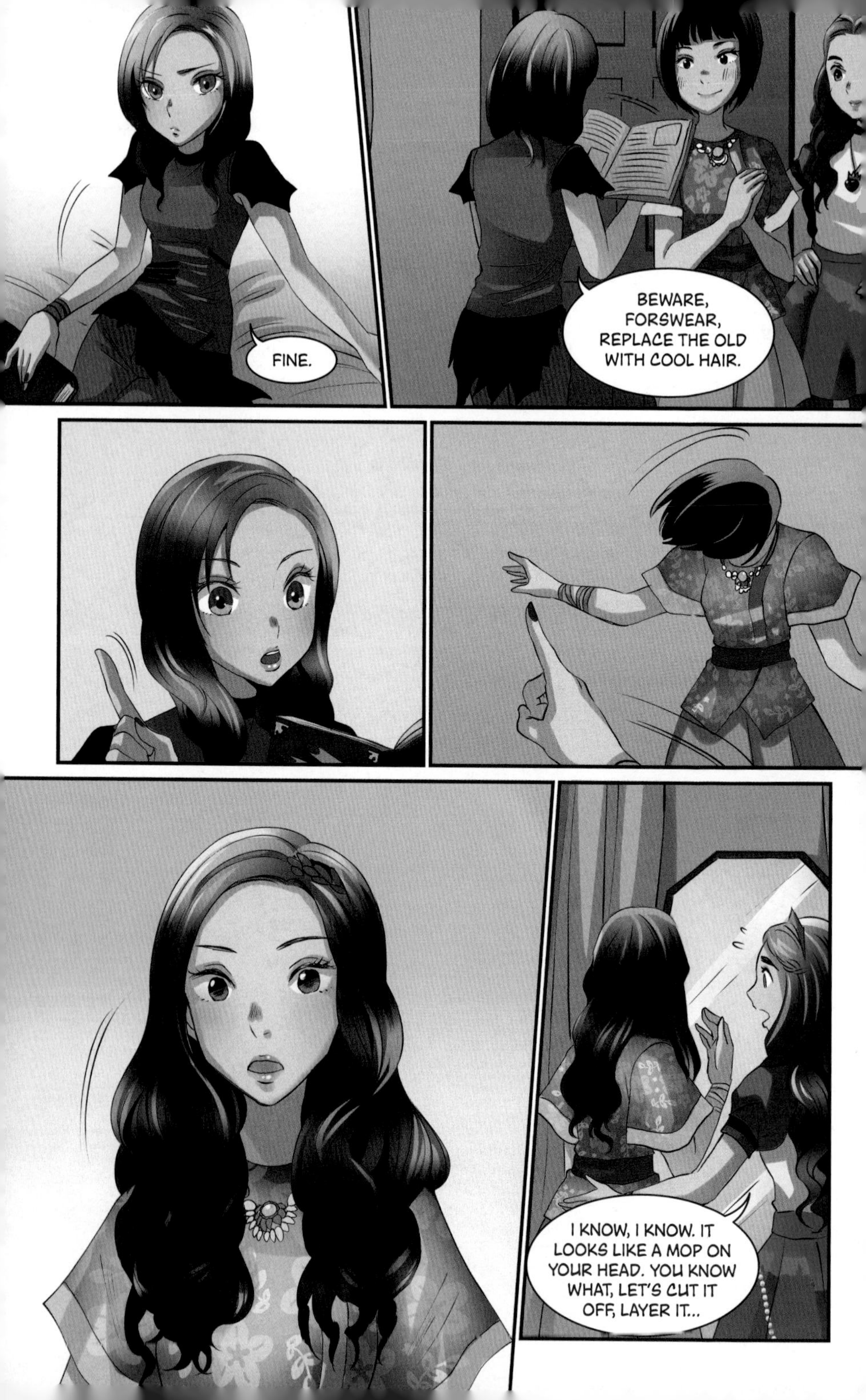
FINE.
BEWARE, FORSWEAR, REPLACE THE OLD WITH COOL HAIR.
I KNOW, I KNOW. IT LOOKS LIKE A MOP ON YOUR HEAD. YOU KNOW WHAT, LET'S CUT IT OFF, LAYER IT...

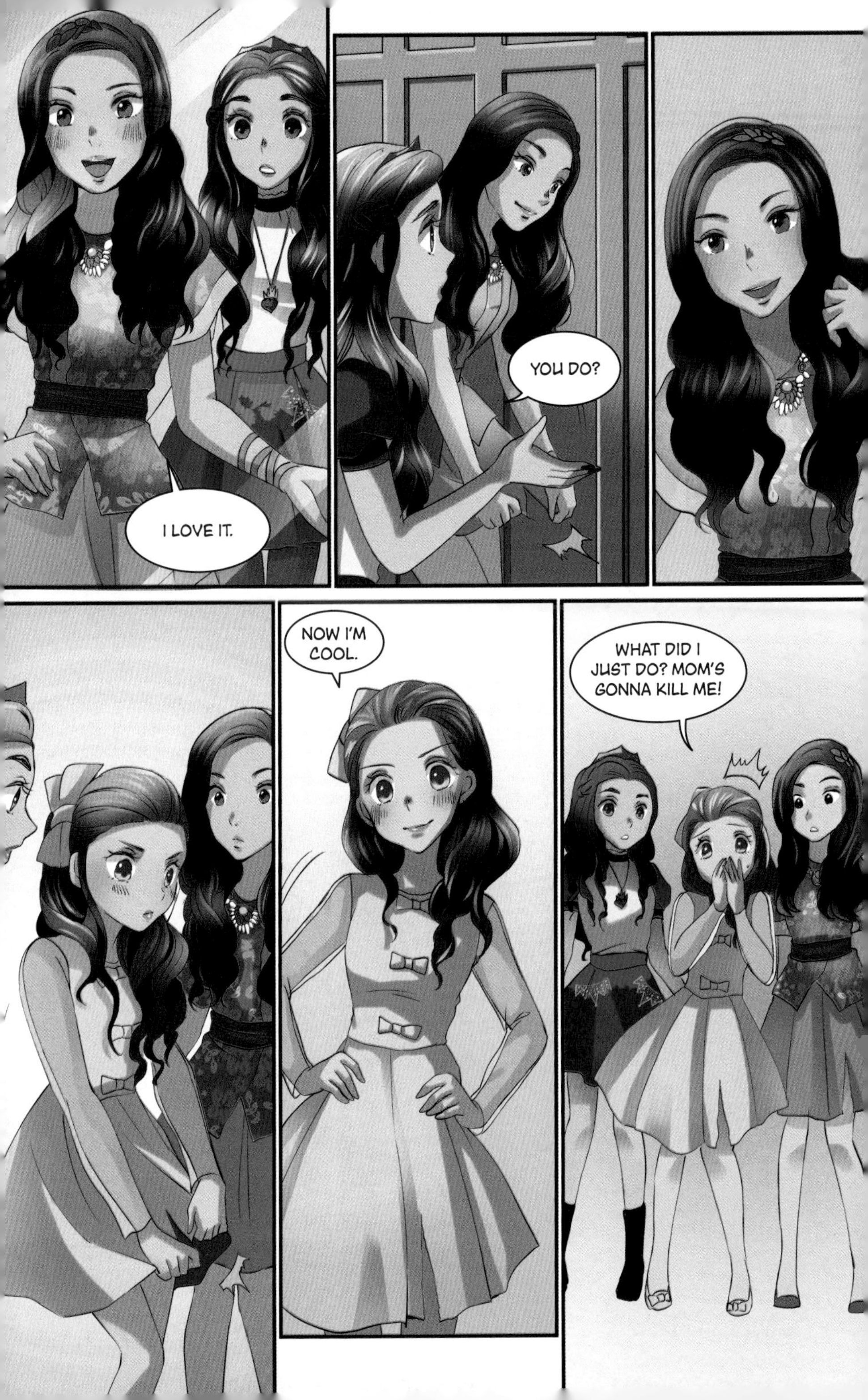
I LOVE IT.
YOU DO?
NOW I'M COOL.
WHAT DID I JUST DO? MOM'S GONNA KILL ME!

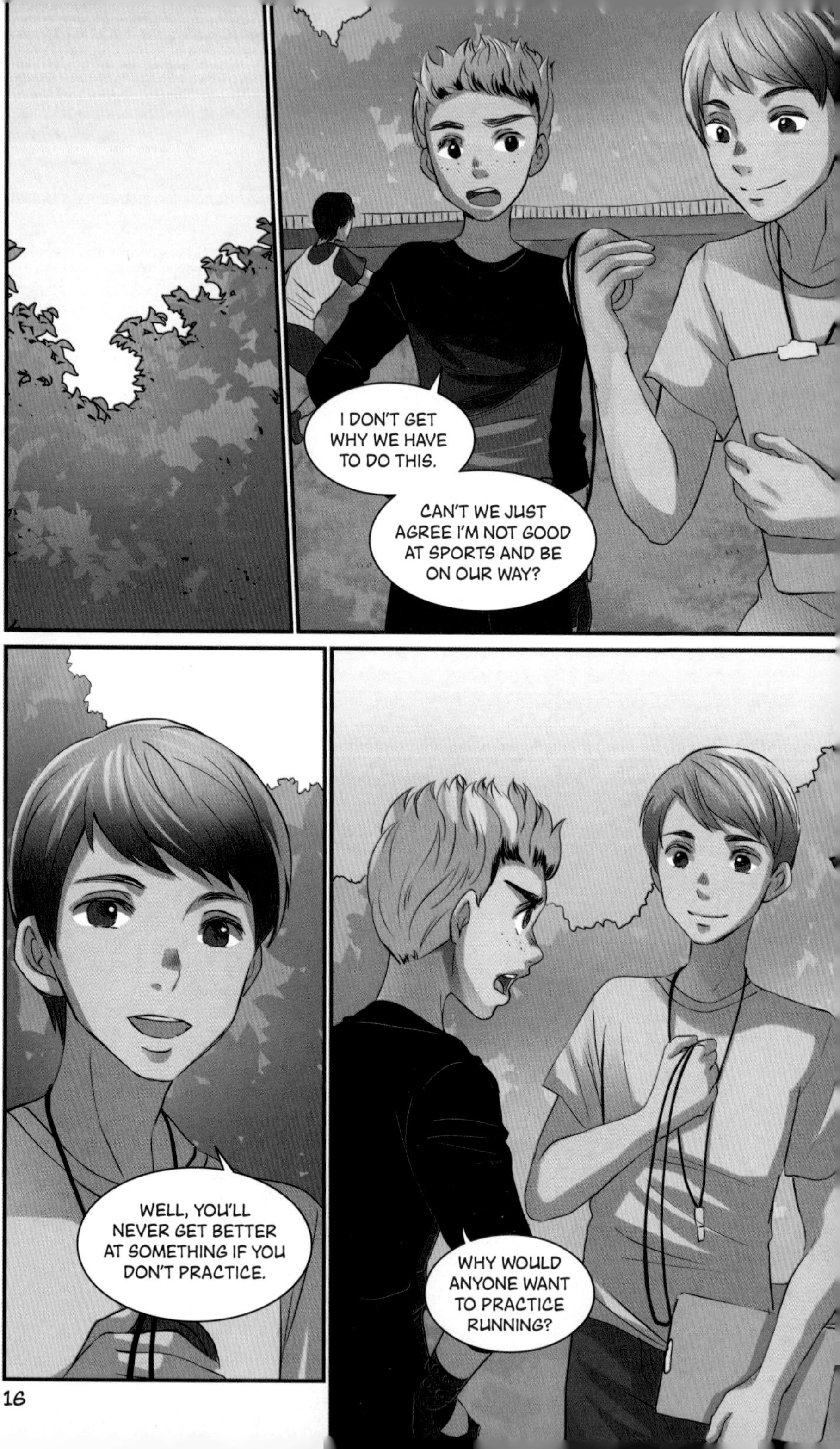
I DON'T GET WHY WE HAVE TO DO THIS.
CAN'T WE JUST AGREE I'M NOT GOOD AT SPORTS AND BE ON OUR WAY?
WELL, YOU'LL NEVER GET BETTER AT SOMETHING IF YOU DON'T PRACTICE.
WHY WOULD ANYONE WANT TO PRACTICE RUNNING?

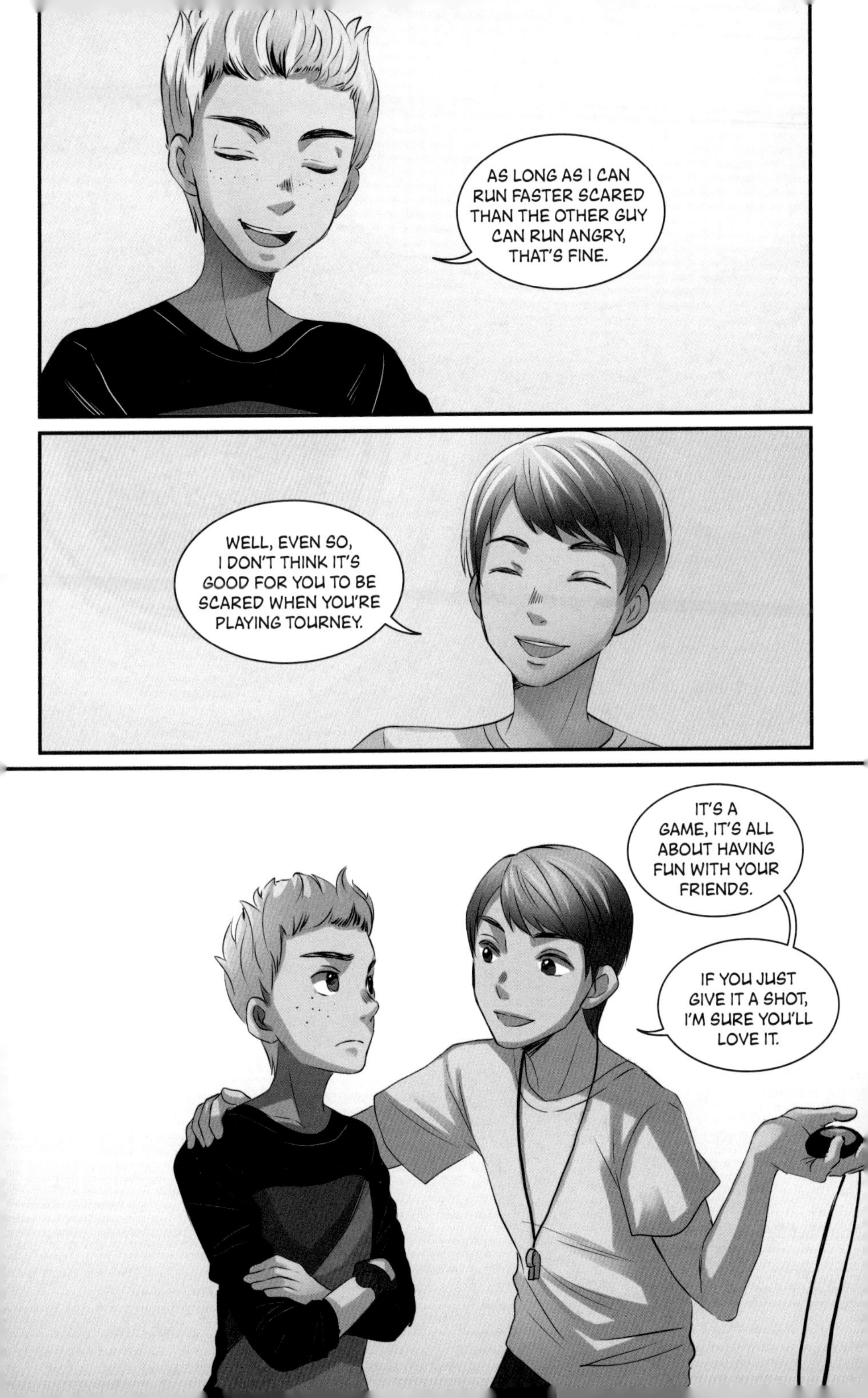
AS LONG AS I CAN RUN FASTER SCARED THAN THE OTHER GUY CAN RUN ANGRY, THAT'S FINE.
WELL, EVEN SO, I DON'T THINK IT'S GOOD FOR YOU TO BE SCARED WHEN YOU'RE PLAYING TOURNEY.
IT'S A GAME, IT'S ALL ABOUT HAVING FUN WITH YOUR FRIENDS.
IF YOU JUST GIVE IT A SHOT, I'M SURE YOU'LL LOVE IT.

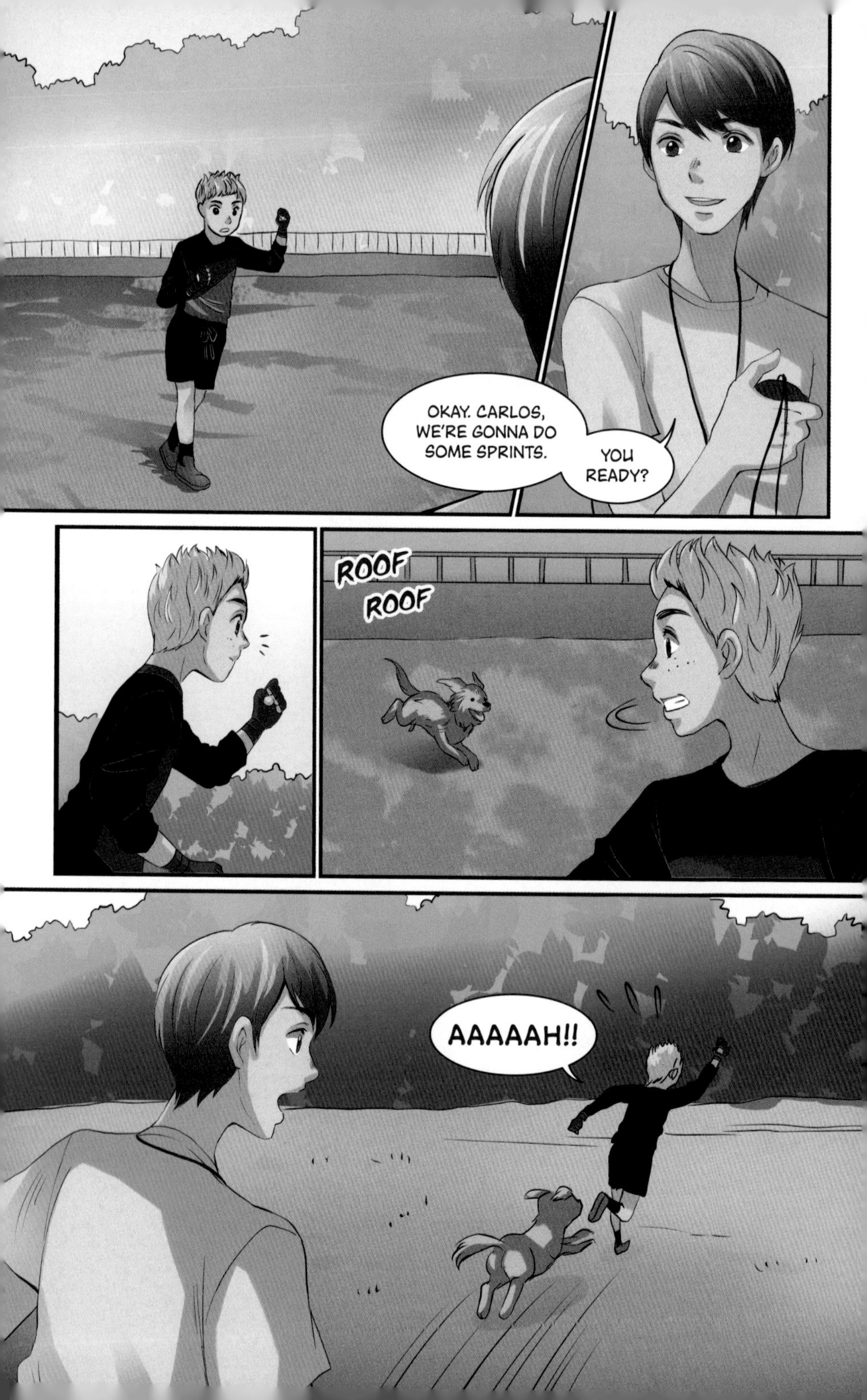
OKAY. CARLOS, WE'RE GONNA DO SOME SPRINTS.
YOU READY?
ROOF
ROOF
AAAAAH!!

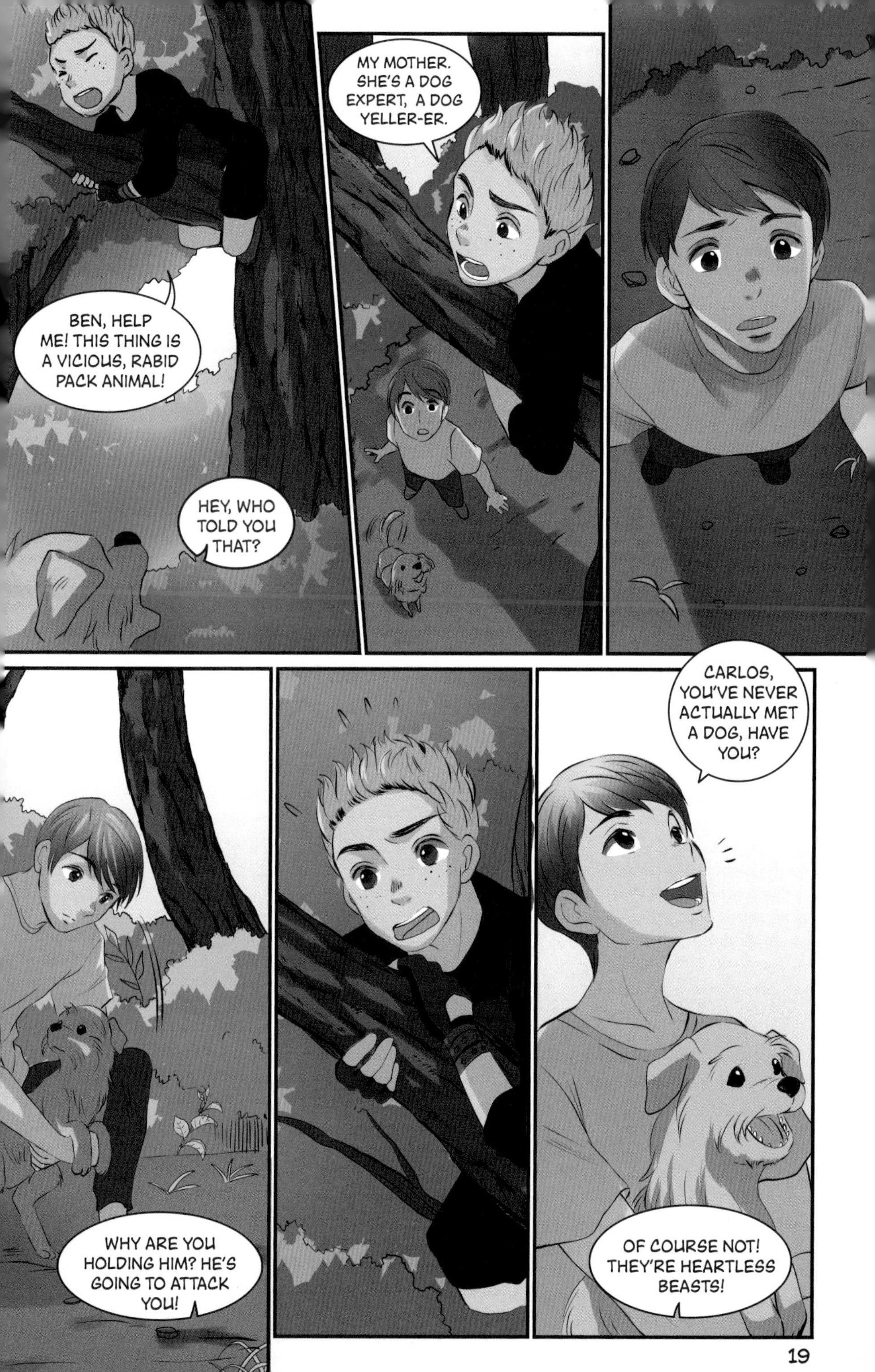
BEN, HELP ME! THIS THING IS A VICIOUS, RABID PACK ANIMAL!
HEY, WHO TOLD YOU THAT?
MY MOTHER. SHE'S A DOG EXPERT, A DOG YELLER-ER.
WHY ARE YOU HOLDING HIM? HE'S GOING TO ATTACK YOU!
CARLOS, YOU'VE NEVER ACTUALLY MET A DOG, HAVE YOU?
OF COURSE NOT! THEY'RE HEARTLESS BEASTS!

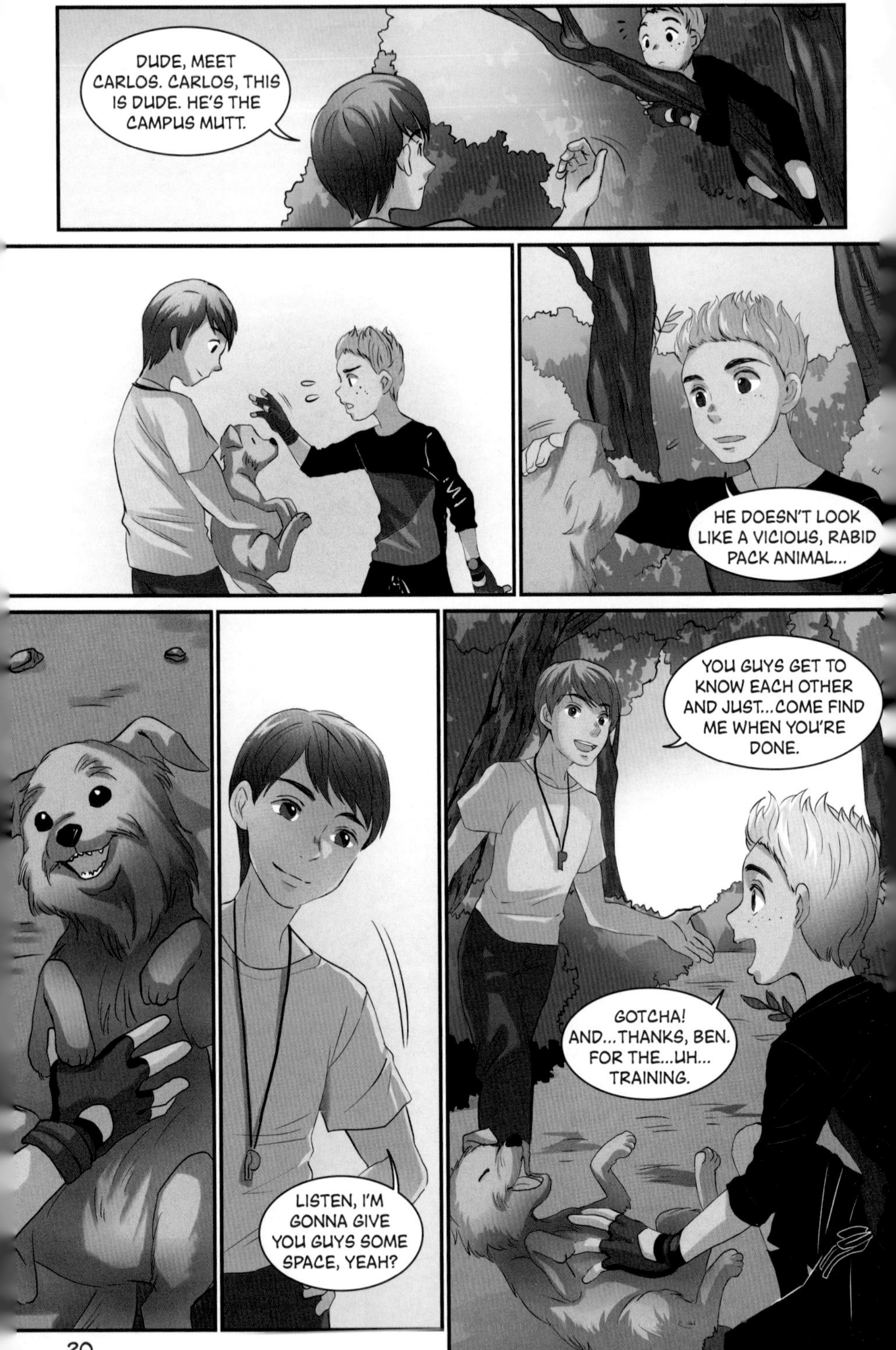
DUDE, MEET CARLOS. CARLOS, THIS IS DUDE. HE'S THE CAMPUS MUTT.
HE DOESN'T LOOK LIKE A VICIOUS, RABID PACK ANIMAL...
LISTEN, I'M GONNA GIVE YOU GUYS SOME SPACE, YEAH?
YOU GUYS GET TO KNOW EACH OTHER AND JUST...COME FIND ME WHEN YOU'RE DONE.
GOTCHA! AND...THANKS, BEN. FOR THE...UH... TRAINING.

Chapter Six
Plan B is for Ben

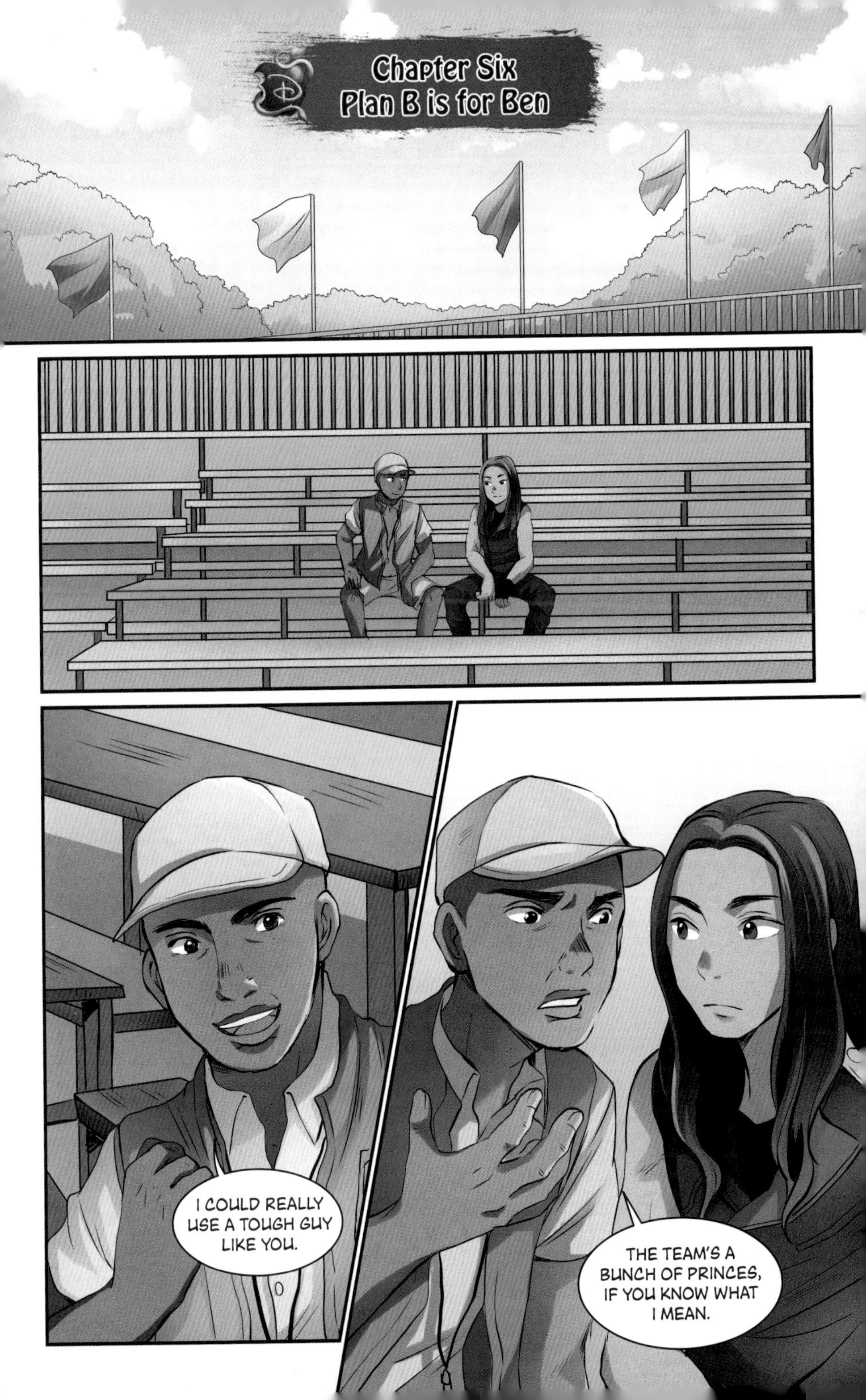
I COULD REALLY USE A TOUGH GUY LIKE YOU.
THE TEAM'S A BUNCH OF PRINCES, IF YOU KNOW WHAT I MEAN.

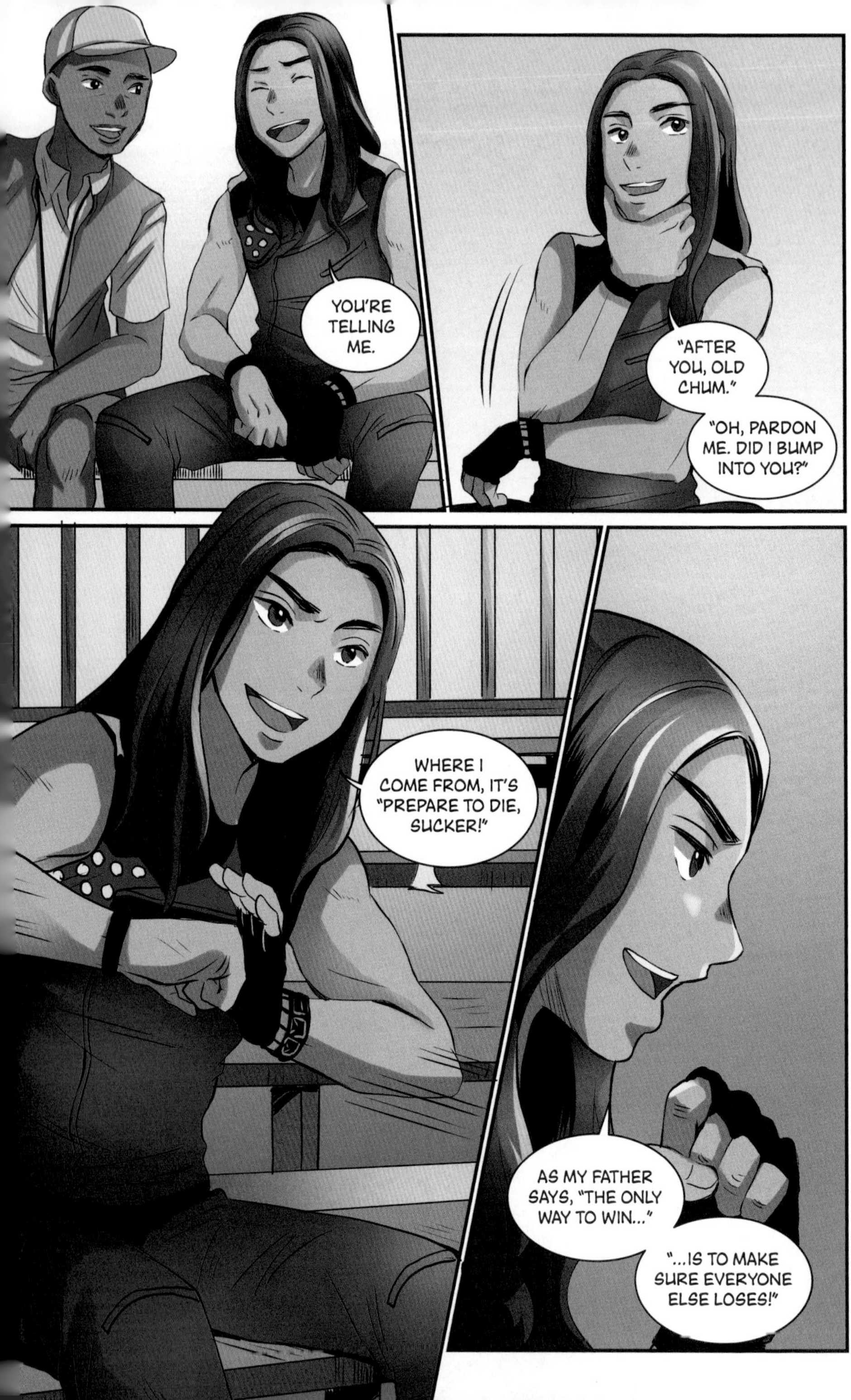
YOU'RE TELLING ME.
"AFTER YOU, OLD CHUM."
"OH, PARDON ME. DID I BUMP INTO YOU?"
WHERE I COME FROM, IT'S "PREPARE TO DIE, SUCKER!"
AS MY FATHER SAYS, "THE ONLY WAY TO WIN..."
"...IS TO MAKE SURE EVERYONE ELSE LOSES!"

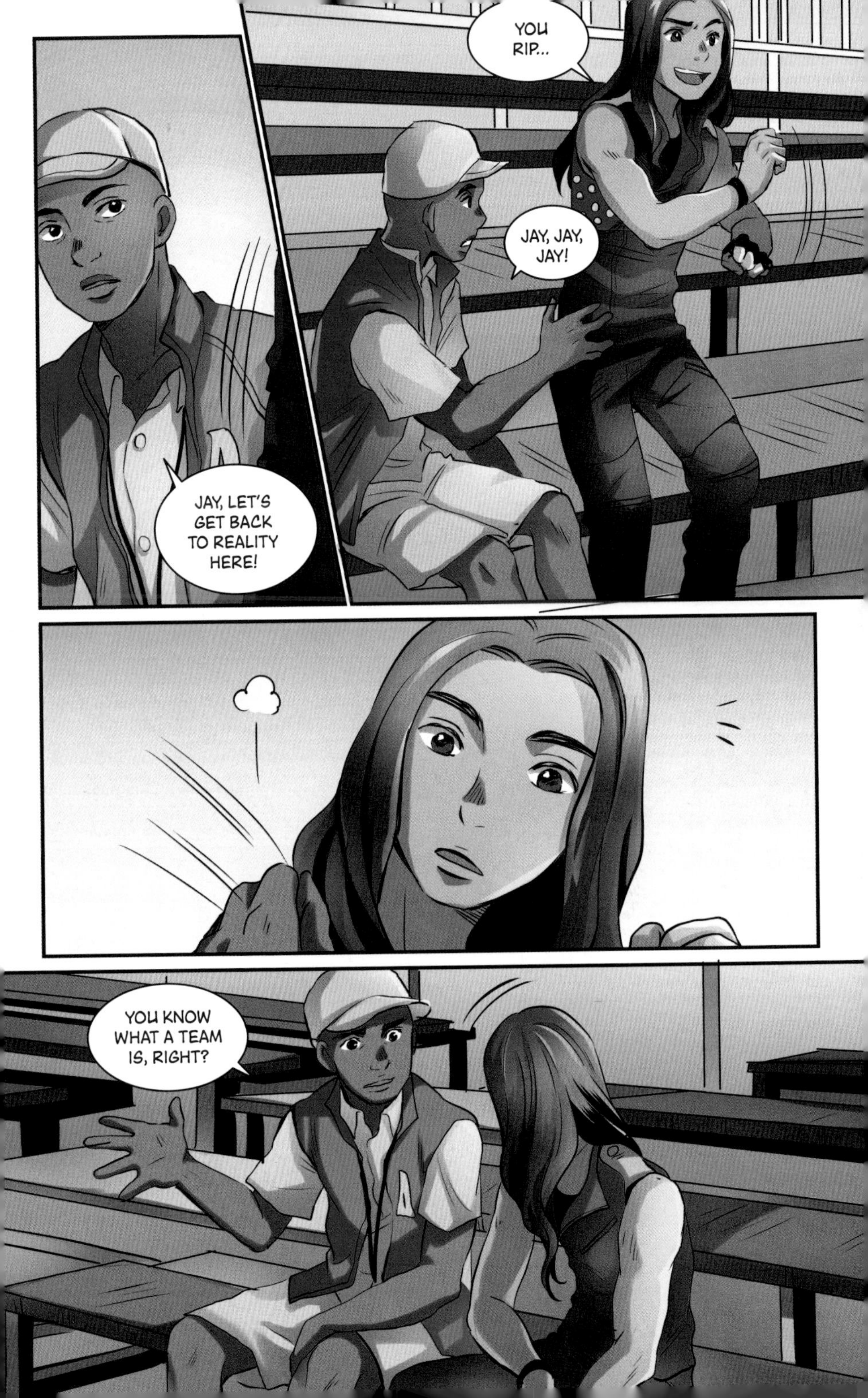
JAY, LET'S GET BACK TO REALITY HERE!
YOU RIP...
JAY, JAY, JAY!
YOU KNOW WHAT A TEAM IS, RIGHT?

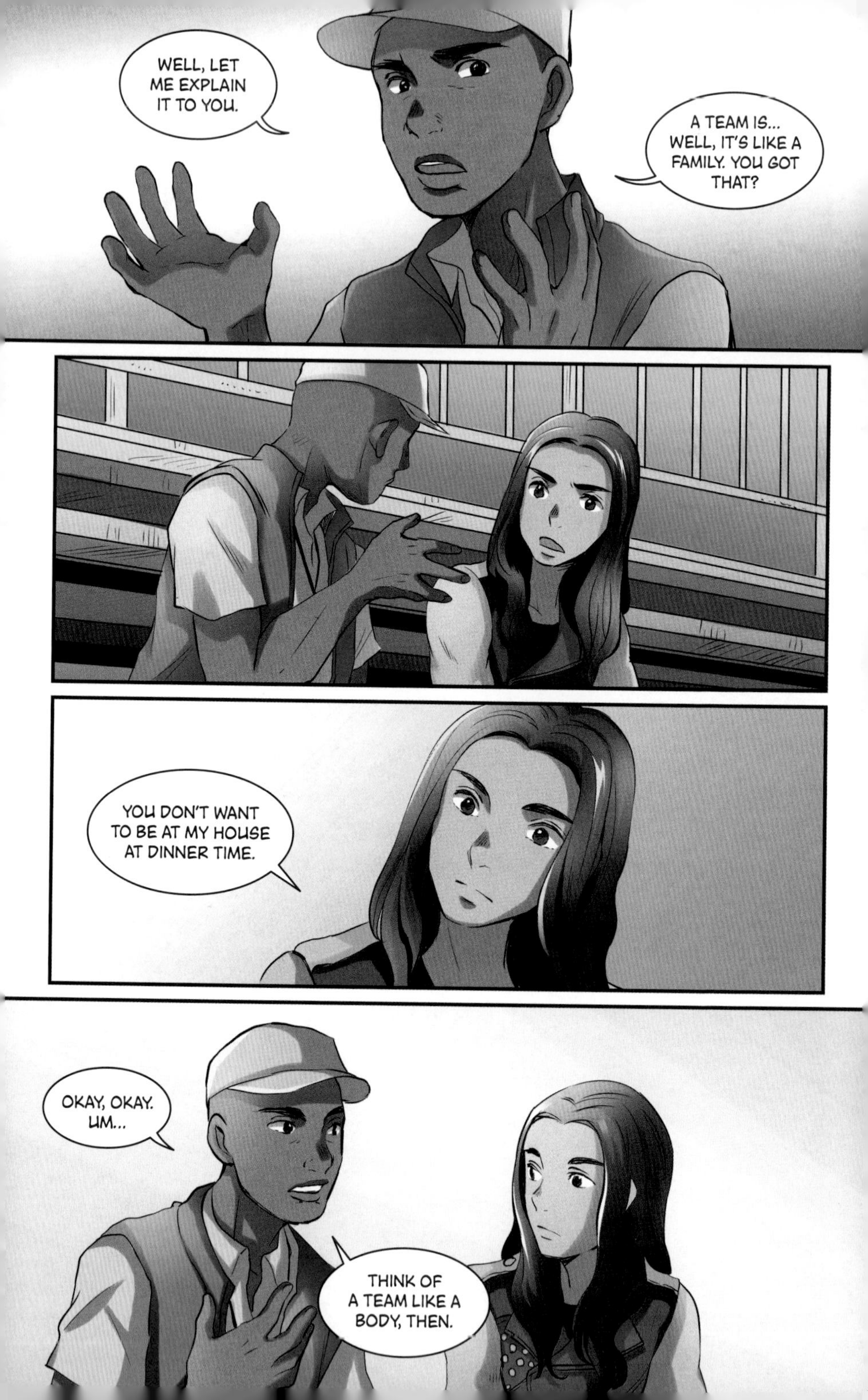
WELL, LET ME EXPLAIN IT TO YOU.
A TEAM IS... WELL, IT'S LIKE A FAMILY. YOU GOT THAT?
YOU DON'T WANT TO BE AT MY HOUSE AT DINNER TIME.
OKAY, OKAY. UM...
THINK OF A TEAM LIKE A BODY, THEN.

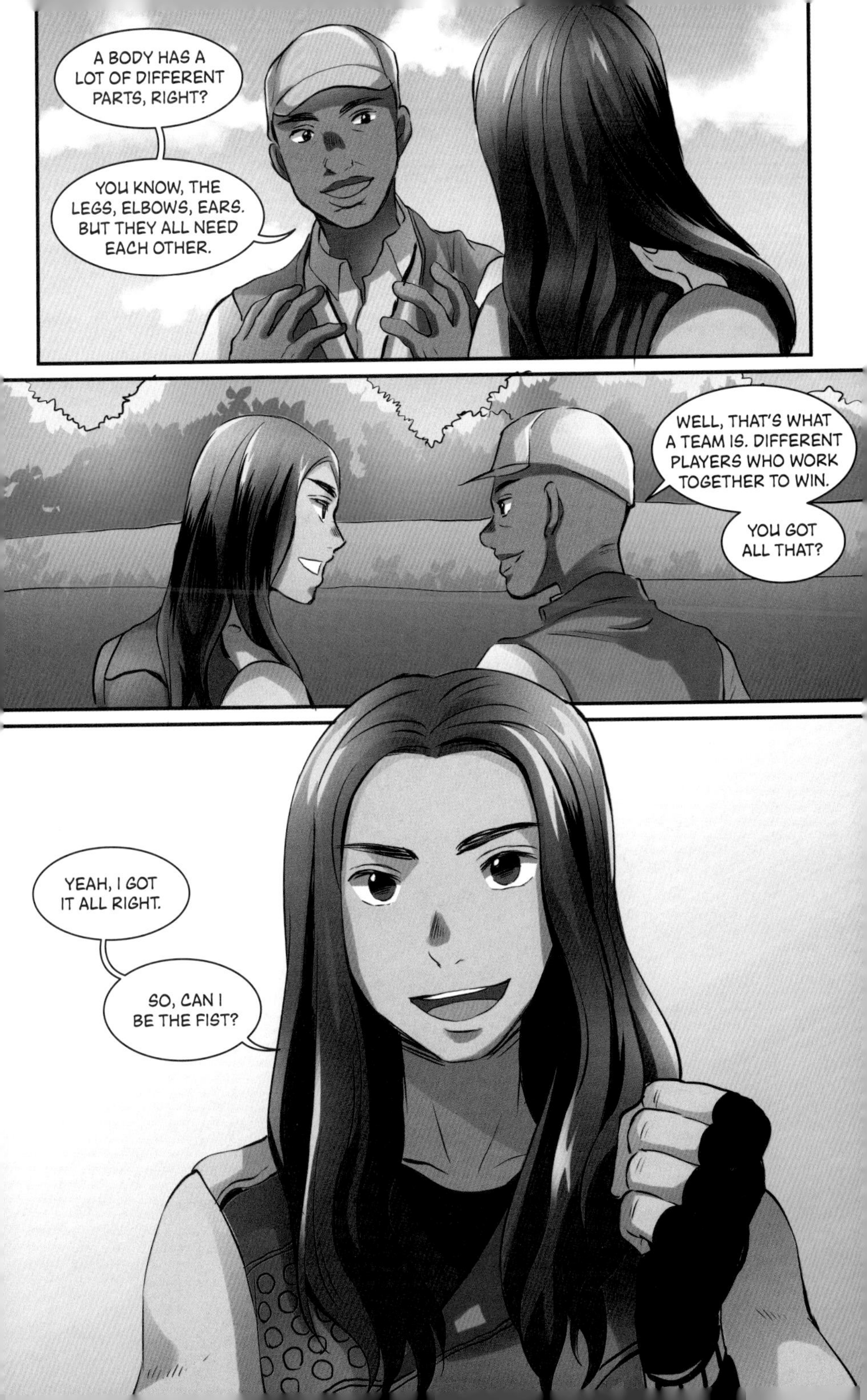
A BODY HAS A LOT OF DIFFERENT PARTS, RIGHT?
YOU KNOW, THE LEGS, ELBOWS, EARS. BUT THEY ALL NEED EACH OTHER.
WELL, THAT'S WHAT A TEAM IS. DIFFERENT PLAYERS WHO WORK TOGETHER TO WIN.
YOU GOT ALL THAT?
YEAH, I GOT IT ALL RIGHT.
SO, CAN I BE THE FIST?

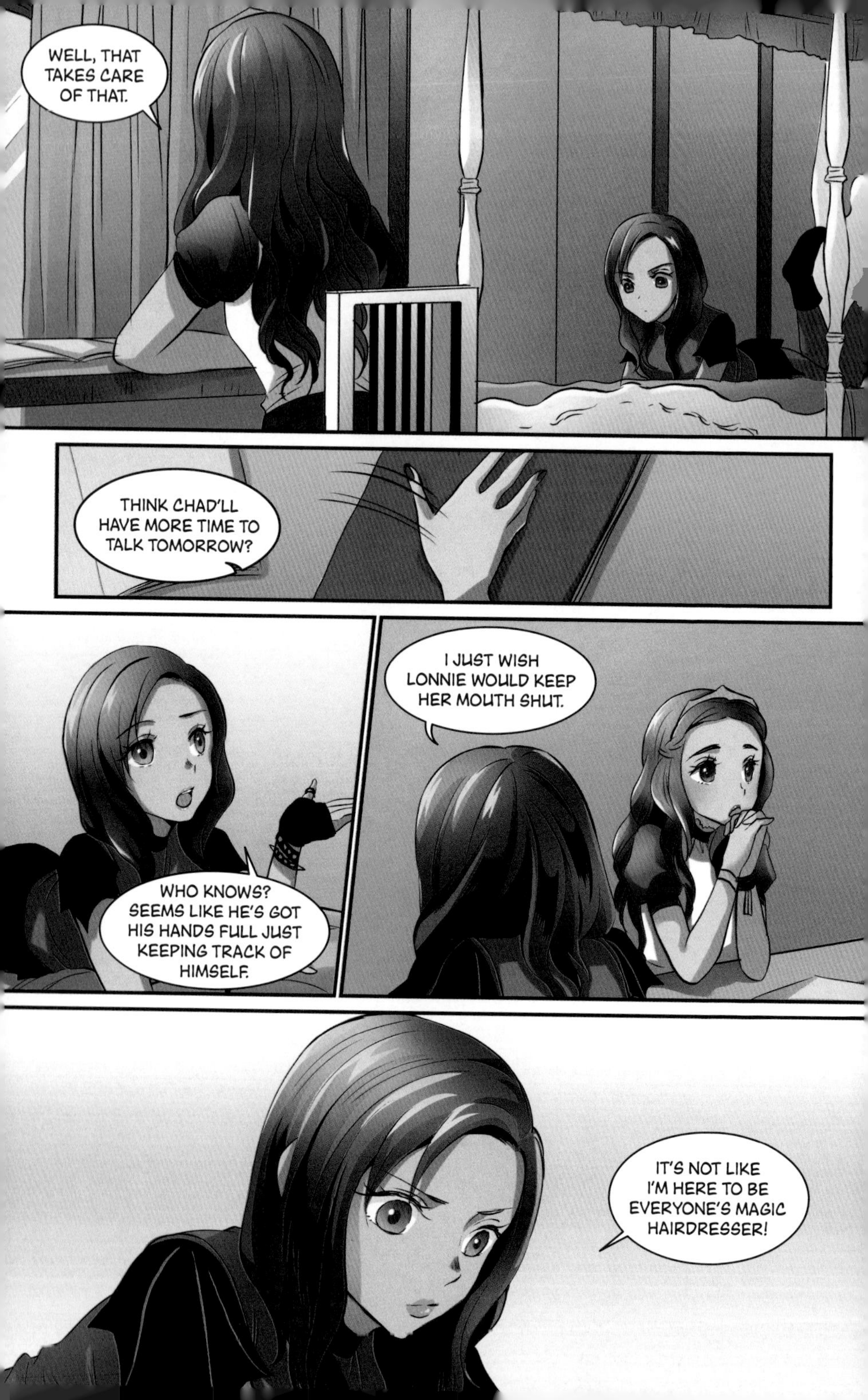
WELL, THAT TAKES CARE OF THAT.
THINK CHAD'LL HAVE MORE TIME TO TALK TOMORROW?
WHO KNOWS? SEEMS LIKE HE'S GOT HIS HANDS FULL JUST KEEPING TRACK OF HIMSELF.
I JUST WISH LONNIE WOULD KEEP HER MOUTH SHUT.
IT'S NOT LIKE I'M HERE TO BE EVERYONE'S MAGIC HAIRDRESSER!

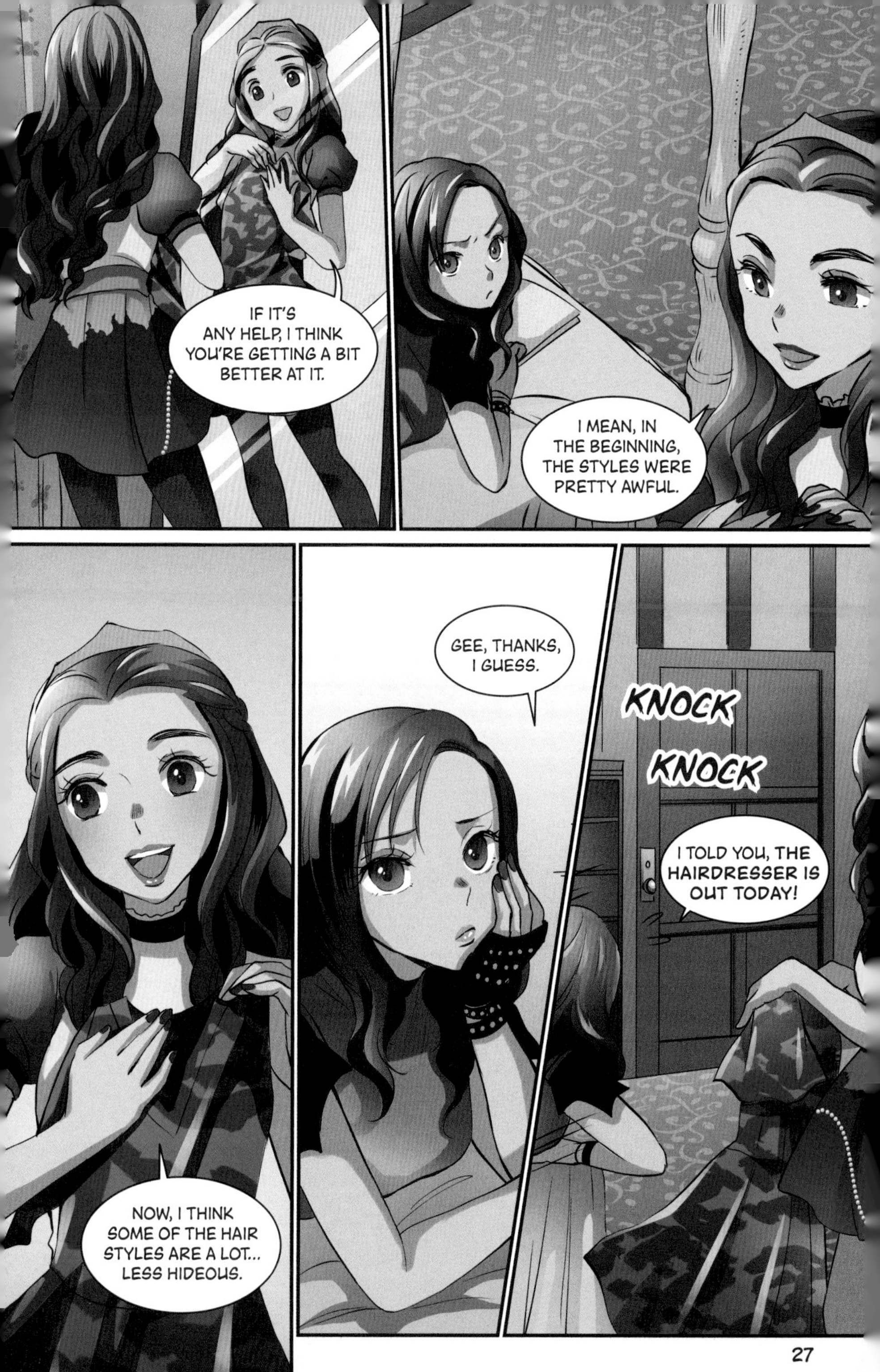
IF IT'S ANY HELP, I THINK YOU'RE GETTING A BIT BETTER AT IT.
I MEAN, IN THE BEGINNING, THE STYLES WERE PRETTY AWFUL.
NOW, I THINK SOME OF THE HAIR STYLES ARE A LOT... LESS HIDEOUS.
GEE, THANKS, I GUESS.
KNOCK
KNOCK
I TOLD YOU, THE HAIRDRESSER IS OUT TODAY!

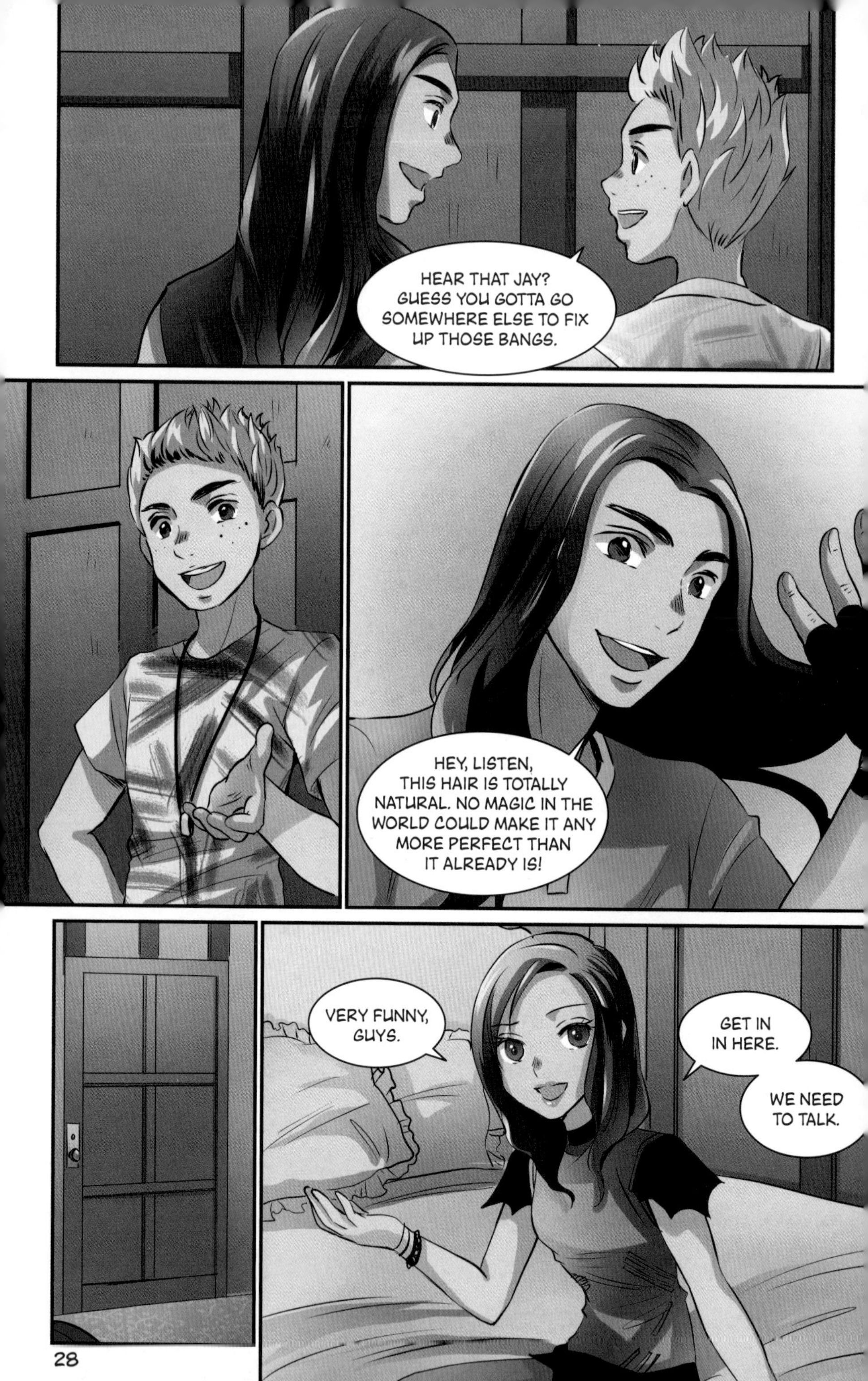
HEAR THAT JAY? GUESS YOU GOTTA GO SOMEWHERE ELSE TO FIX UP THOSE BANGS.
HEY, LISTEN, THIS HAIR IS TOTALLY NATURAL. NO MAGIC IN THE WORLD COULD MAKE IT ANY MORE PERFECT THAN IT ALREADY IS!
VERY FUNNY, GUYS.
GET IN IN HERE.
WE NEED TO TALK.

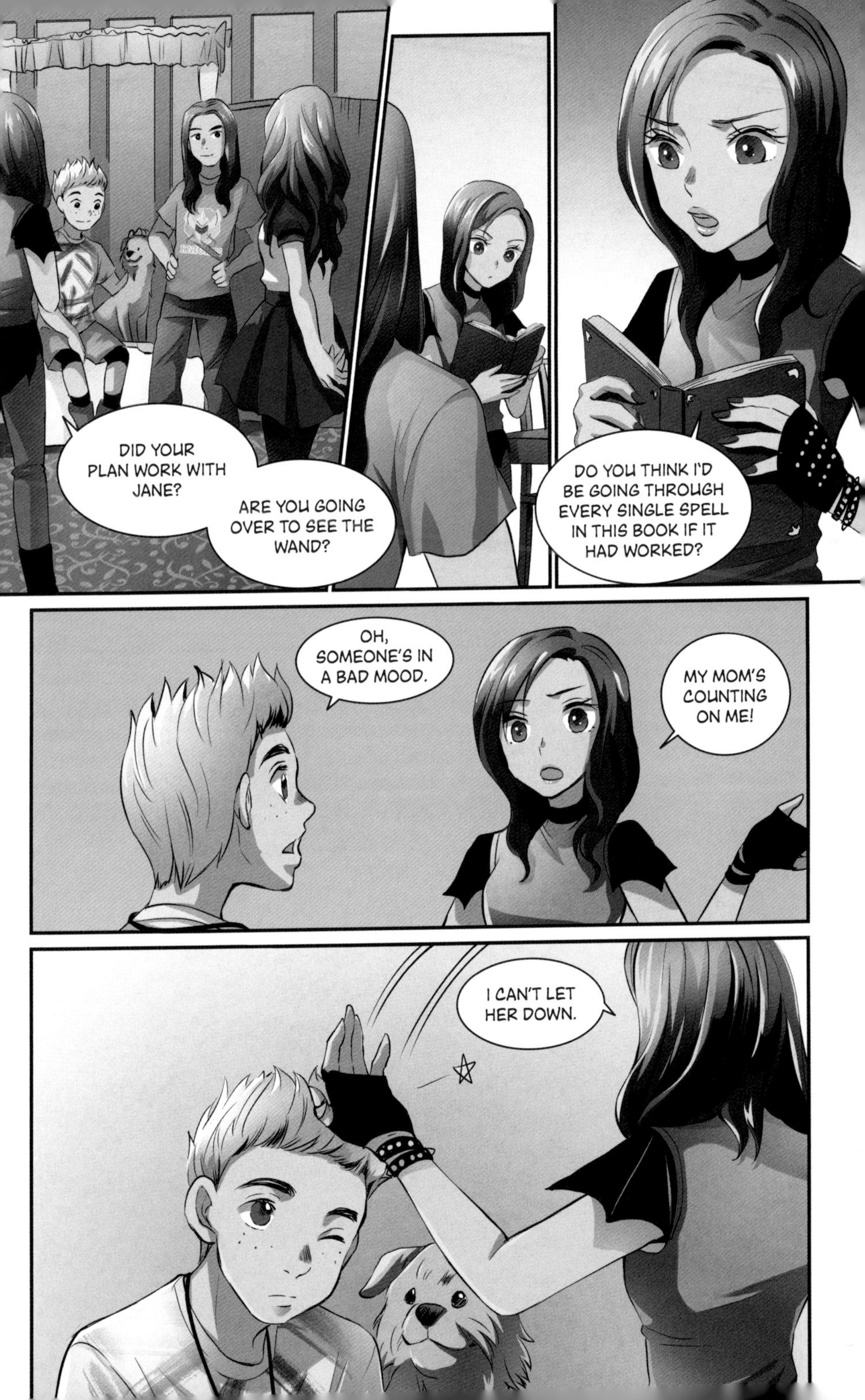
DID YOUR PLAN WORK WITH JANE?
ARE YOU GOING OVER TO SEE THE WAND?
DO YOU THINK I'D BE GOING THROUGH EVERY SINGLE SPELL IN THIS BOOK IF IT HAD WORKED?
OH, SOMEONE'S IN A BAD MOOD.
MY MOM'S COUNTING ON ME!
I CAN'T LET HER DOWN.

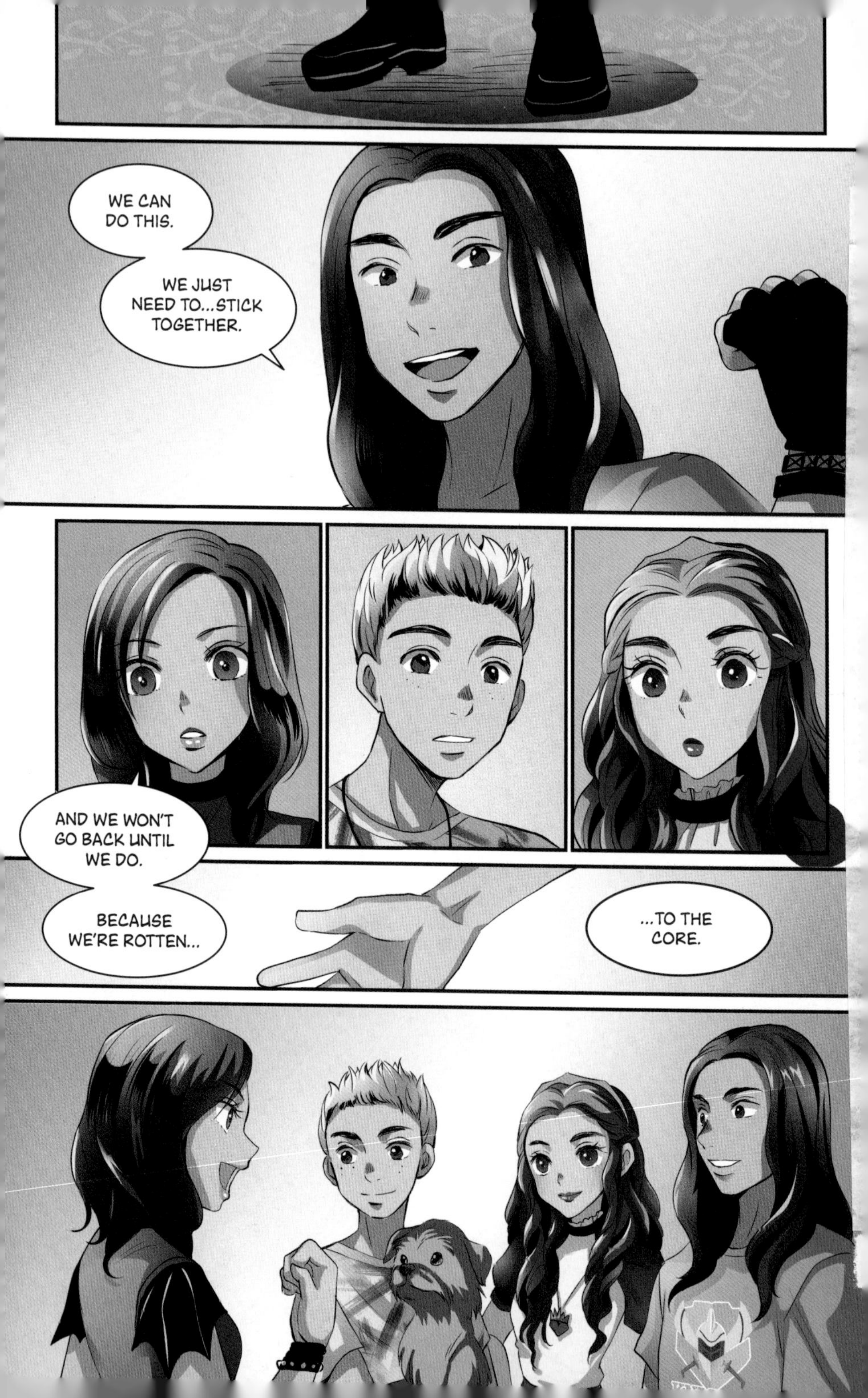
WE CAN DO THIS.
WE JUST NEED TO...STICK TOGETHER.
AND WE WON'T GO BACK UNTIL WE DO.
BECAUSE WE'RE ROTTEN...
...TO THE CORE.

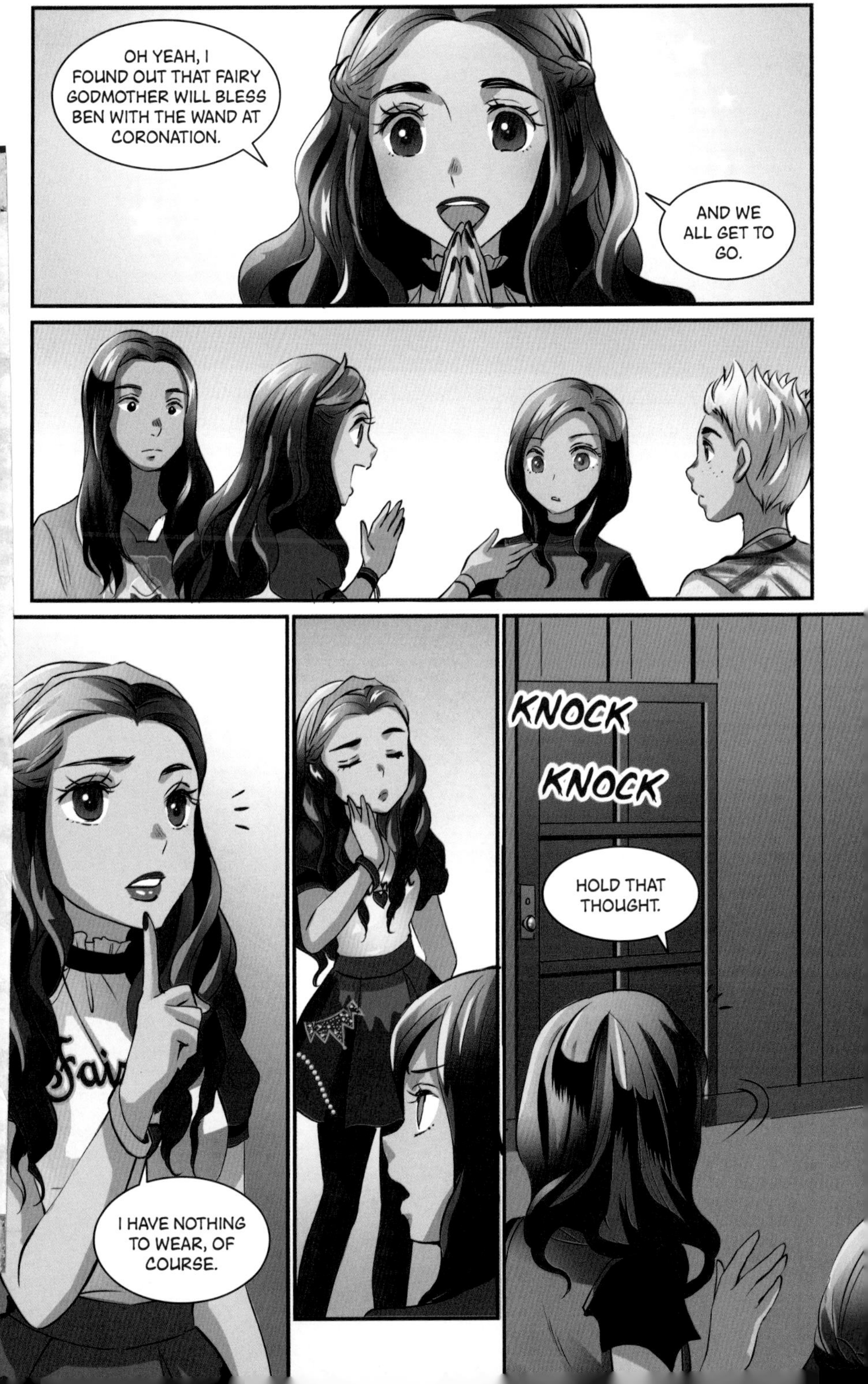
OH YEAH, I FOUND OUT THAT FAIRY GODMOTHER WILL BLESS BEN WITH THE WAND AT CORONATION.
AND WE ALL GET TO GO.
I HAVE NOTHING TO WEAR, OF COURSE.
KNOCK
KNOCK
HOLD THAT THOUGHT.

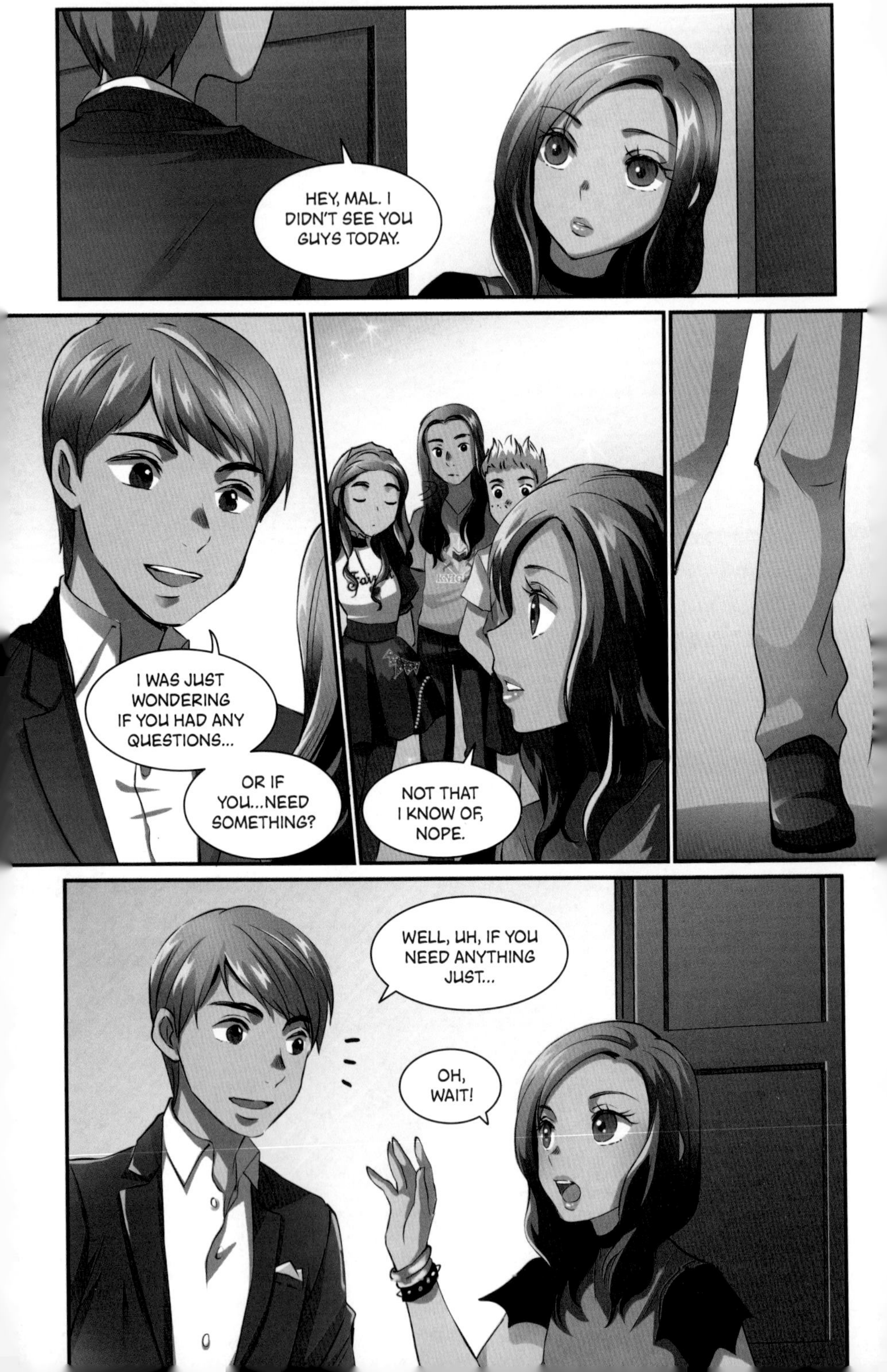
HEY, MAL. I DIDN'T SEE YOU GUYS TODAY.
I WAS JUST WONDERING IF YOU HAD ANY QUESTIONS...
OR IF YOU...NEED SOMETHING?
NOT THAT I KNOW OF, NOPE.
WELL, UH, IF YOU NEED ANYTHING JUST...
OH, WAIT!

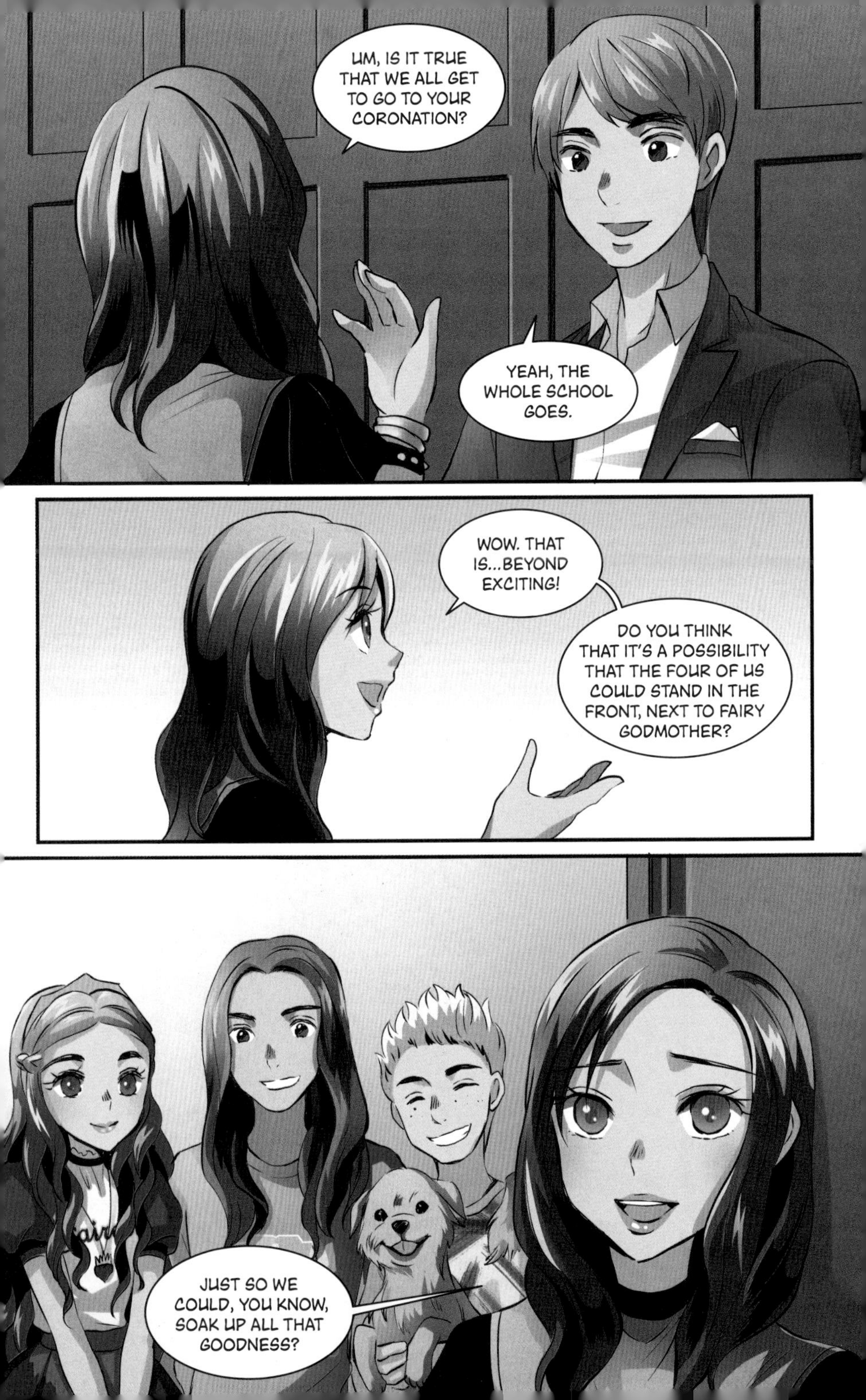
UM, IS IT TRUE THAT WE ALL GET TO GO TO YOUR CORONATION?
YEAH, THE WHOLE SCHOOL GOES.
WOW. THAT IS...BEYOND EXCITING!
DO YOU THINK THAT IT'S A POSSIBILITY THAT THE FOUR OF US COULD STAND IN THE FRONT, NEXT TO FAIRY GODMOTHER?
JUST SO WE COULD, YOU KNOW, SOAK UP ALL THAT GOODNESS?

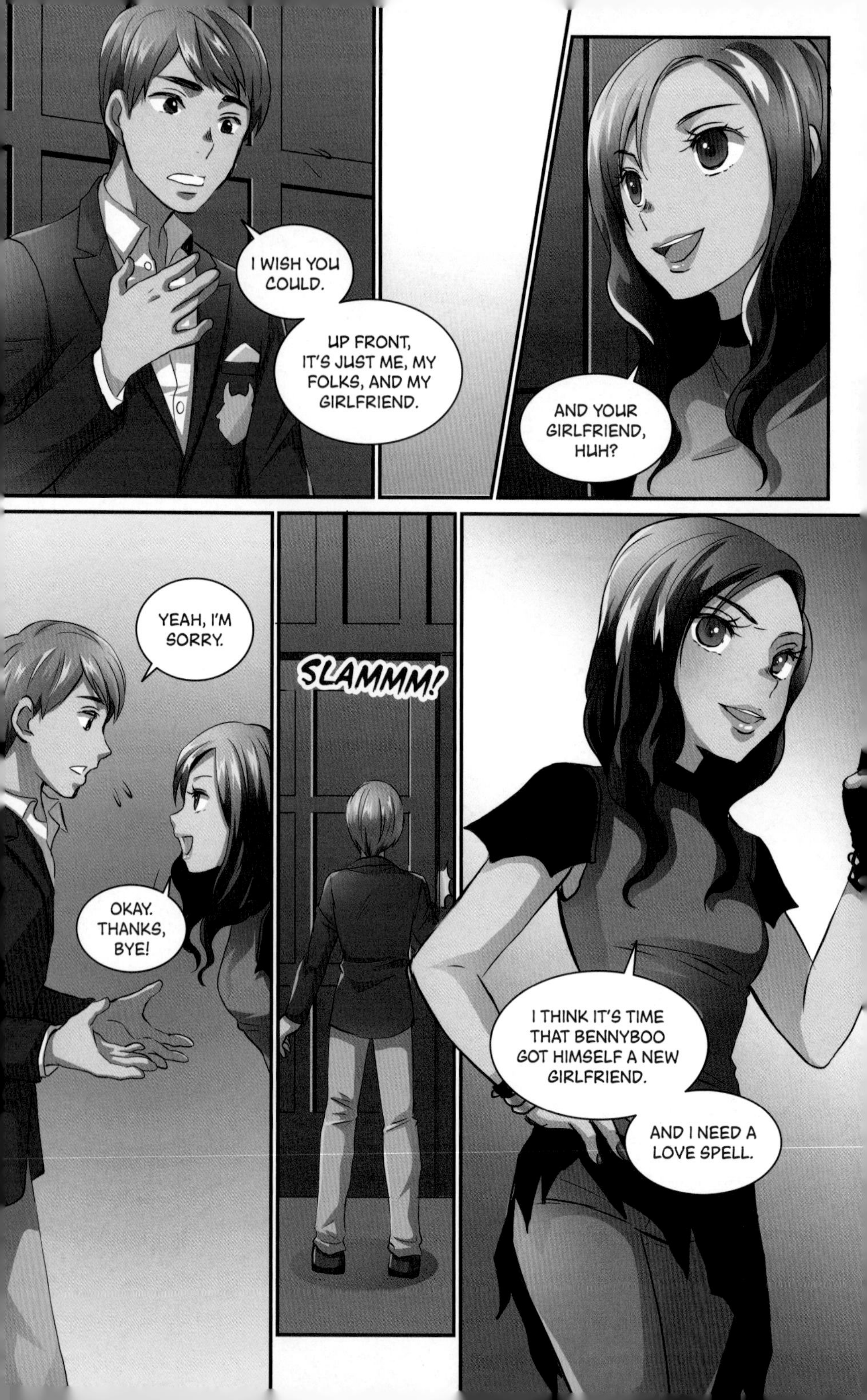
I WISH YOU COULD.
UP FRONT, IT'S JUST ME, MY FOLKS, AND MY GIRLFRIEND.
AND YOUR GIRLFRIEND, HUH?
YEAH, I'M SORRY.
OKAY. THANKS, BYE!
SLAMMM!
I THINK IT'S TIME THAT BENNYBOO GOT HIMSELF A NEW GIRLFRIEND.
AND I NEED A LOVE SPELL.

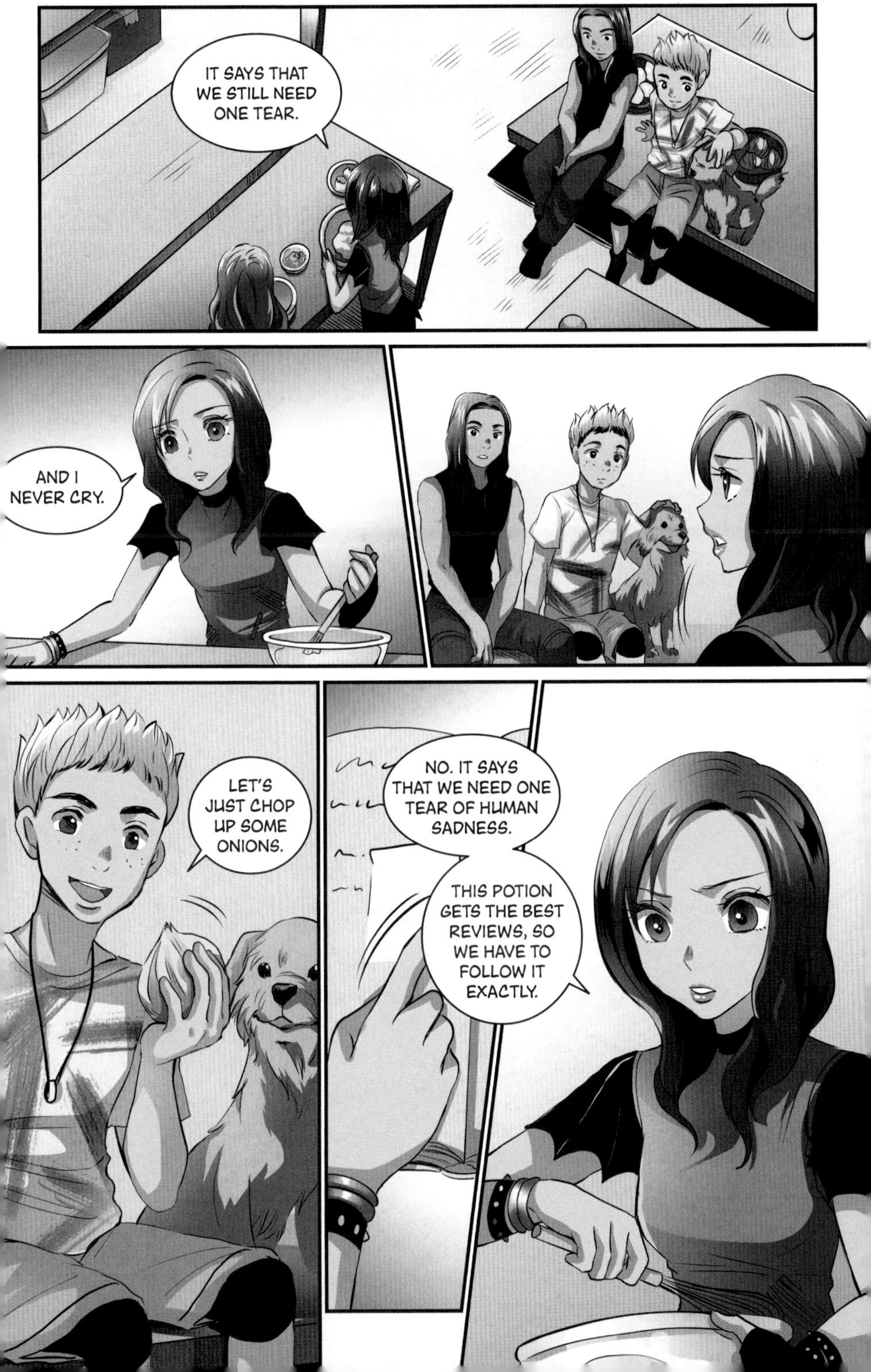
IT SAYS THAT WE STILL NEED ONE TEAR.
AND I NEVER CRY.
LET'S JUST CHOP UP SOME ONIONS.
NO. IT SAYS THAT WE NEED ONE TEAR OF HUMAN SADNESS.
THIS POTION GETS THE BEST REVIEWS, SO WE HAVE TO FOLLOW IT EXACTLY.

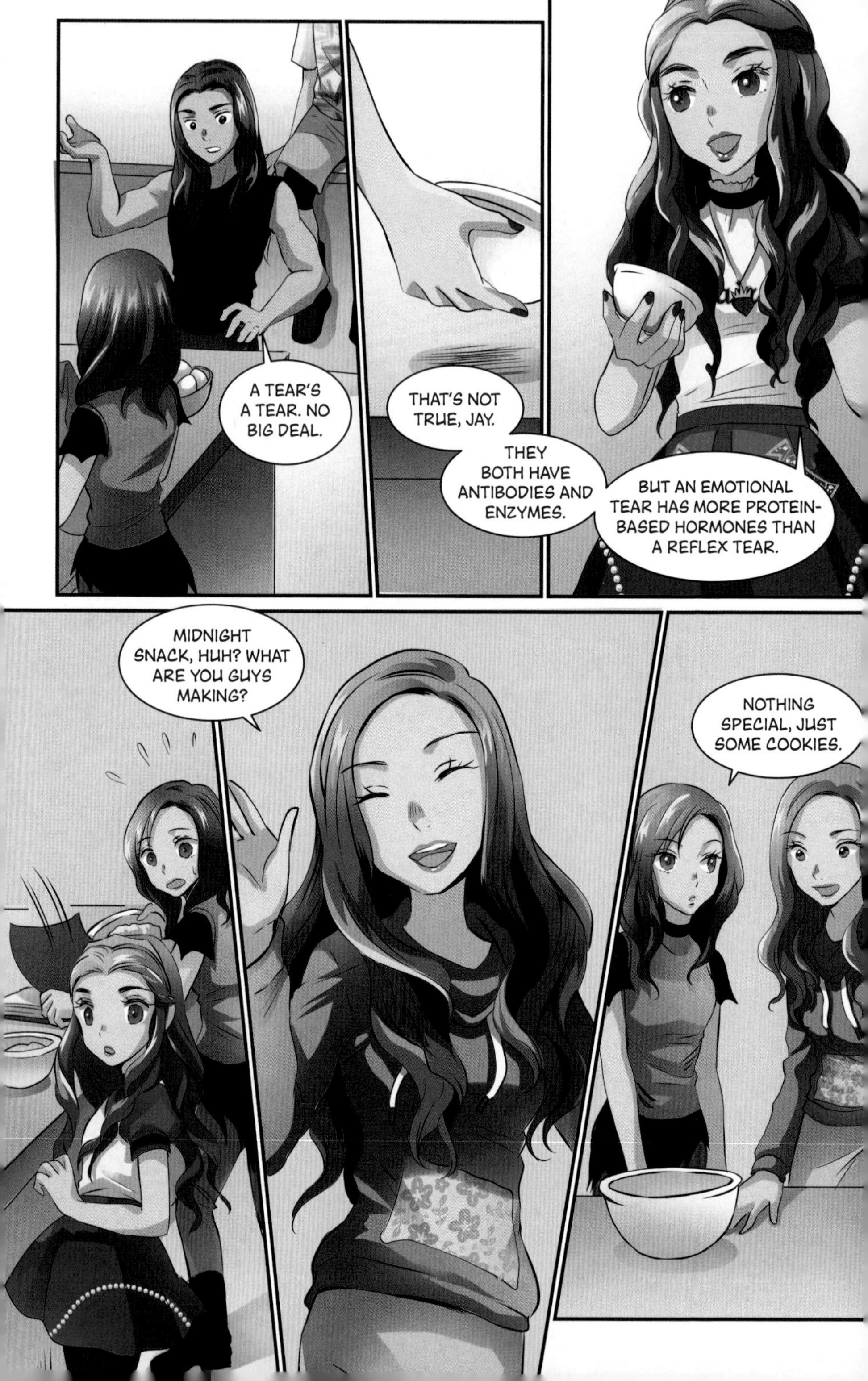
A TEAR'S A TEAR. NO BIG DEAL.
THAT'S NOT TRUE, JAY.
THEY BOTH HAVE ANTIBODIES AND ENZYMES.
BUT AN EMOTIONAL TEAR HAS MORE PROTEIN-BASED HORMONES THAN A REFLEX TEAR.
MIDNIGHT SNACK, HUH? WHAT ARE YOU GUYS MAKING?
NOTHING SPECIAL, JUST SOME COOKIES.

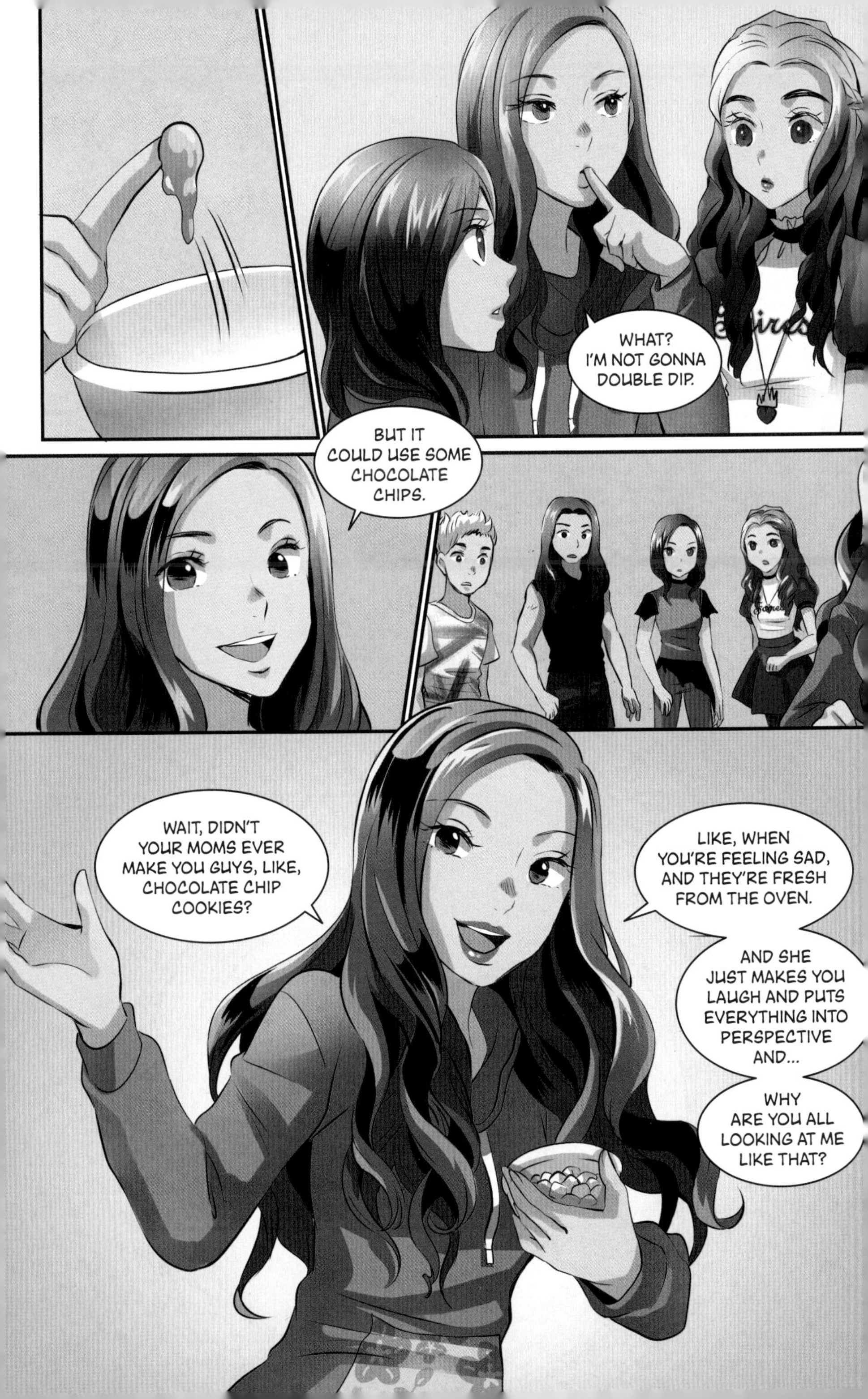
WHAT? I'M NOT GONNA DOUBLE DIP.
BUT IT COULD USE SOME CHOCOLATE CHIPS.
WAIT, DIDN'T YOUR MOMS EVER MAKE YOU GUYS, LIKE, CHOCOLATE CHIP COOKIES?
LIKE, WHEN YOU'RE FEELING SAD, AND THEY'RE FRESH FROM THE OVEN.
AND SHE JUST MAKES YOU LAUGH AND PUTS EVERYTHING INTO PERSPECTIVE AND...
WHY ARE YOU ALL LOOKING AT ME LIKE THAT?

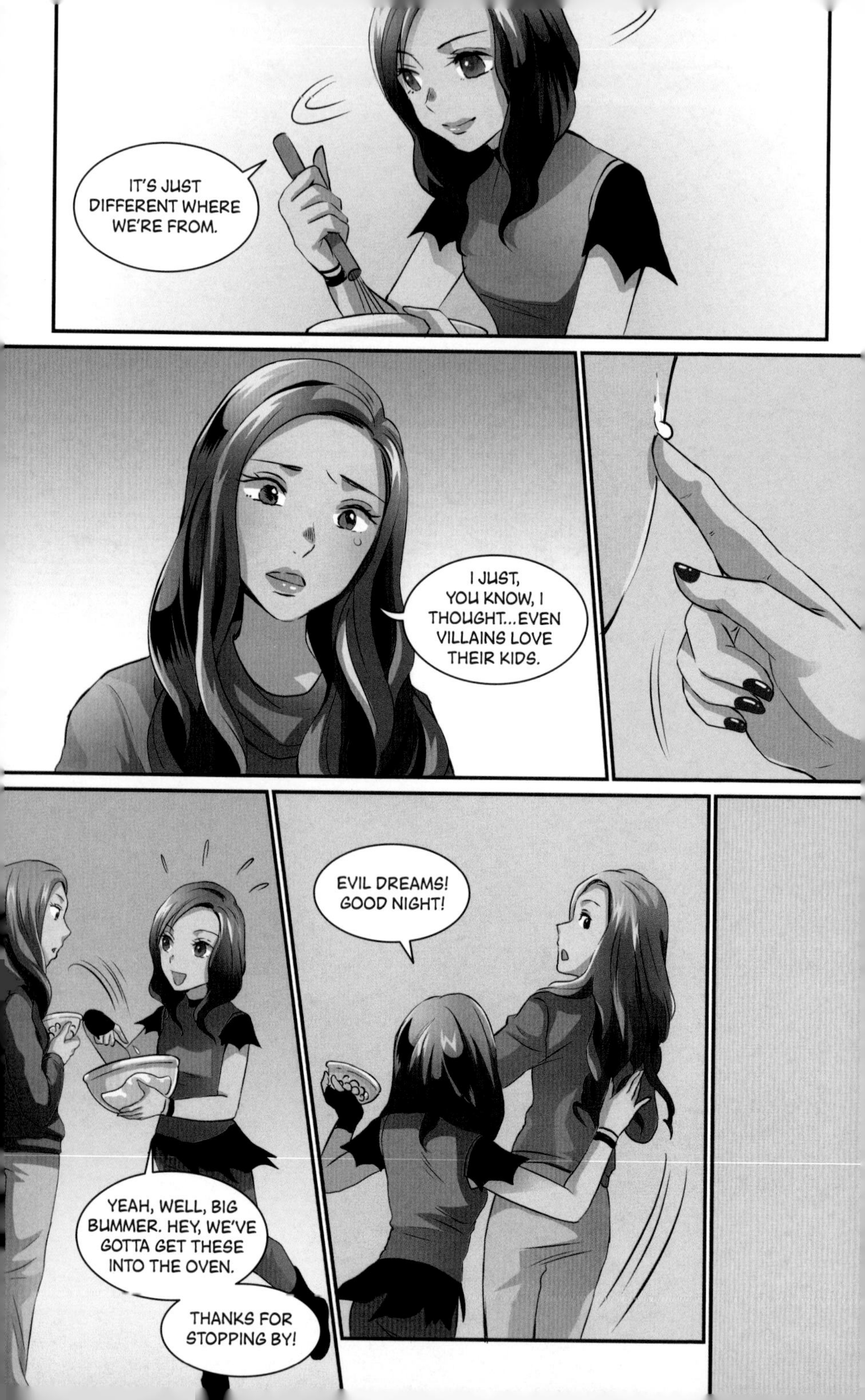
IT'S JUST DIFFERENT WHERE WE'RE FROM.
I JUST, YOU KNOW, I THOUGHT...EVEN VILLAINS LOVE THEIR KIDS.
YEAH, WELL, BIG BUMMER. HEY, WE'VE GOTTA GET THESE INTO THE OVEN.
THANKS FOR STOPPING BY!
EVIL DREAMS! GOOD NIGHT!

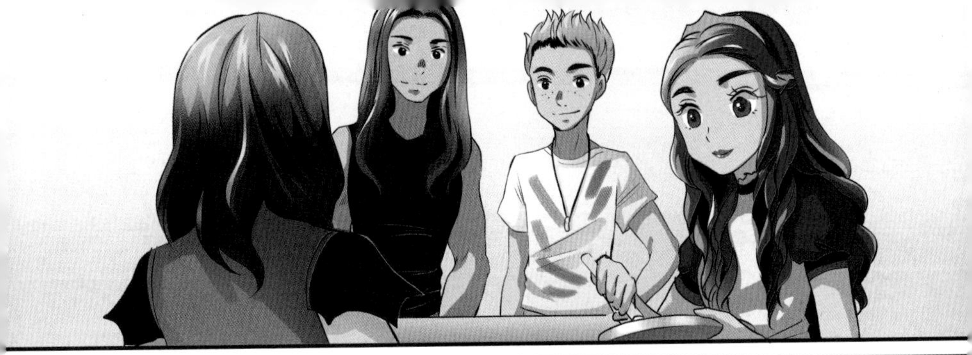
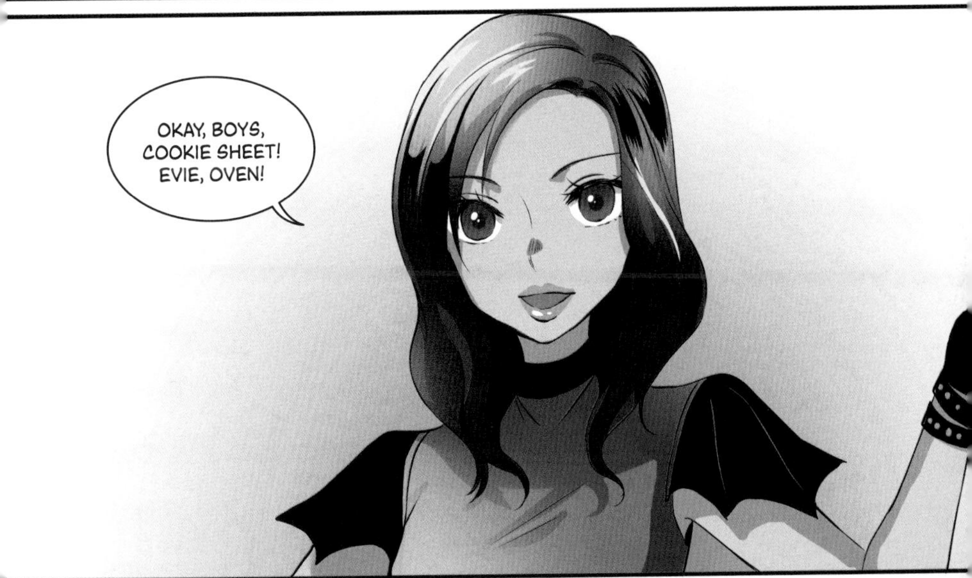
OKAY, BOYS, COOKIE SHEET! EVIE, OVEN!
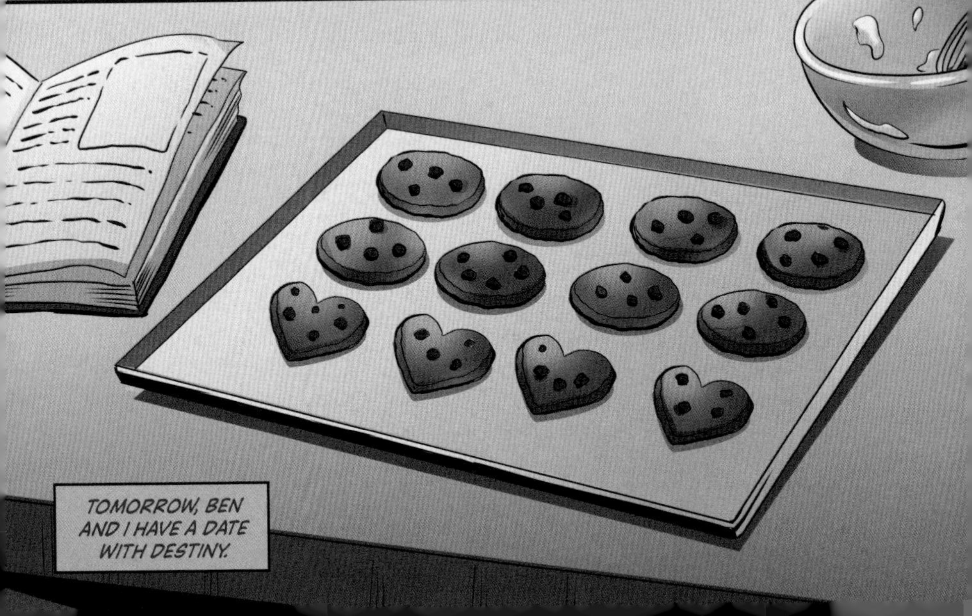
TOMORROW, BEN AND I HAVE A DATE WITH DESTINY.

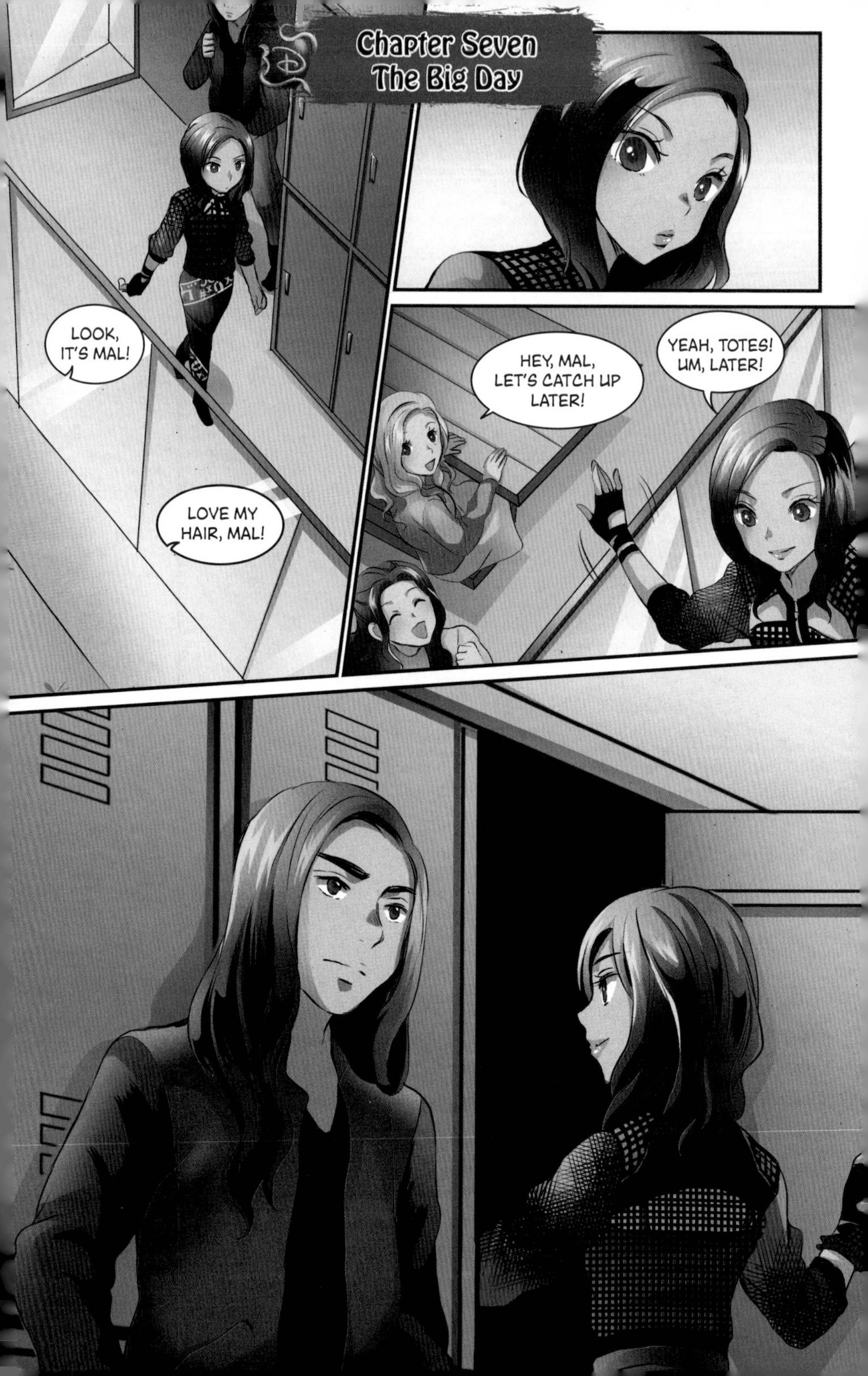
Chapter Seven
The Big Day
LOOK, IT'S MAL!
LOVE MY HAIR, MAL!
HEY, MAL, LET'S CATCH UP LATER!
YEAH, TOTES! UM, LATER!

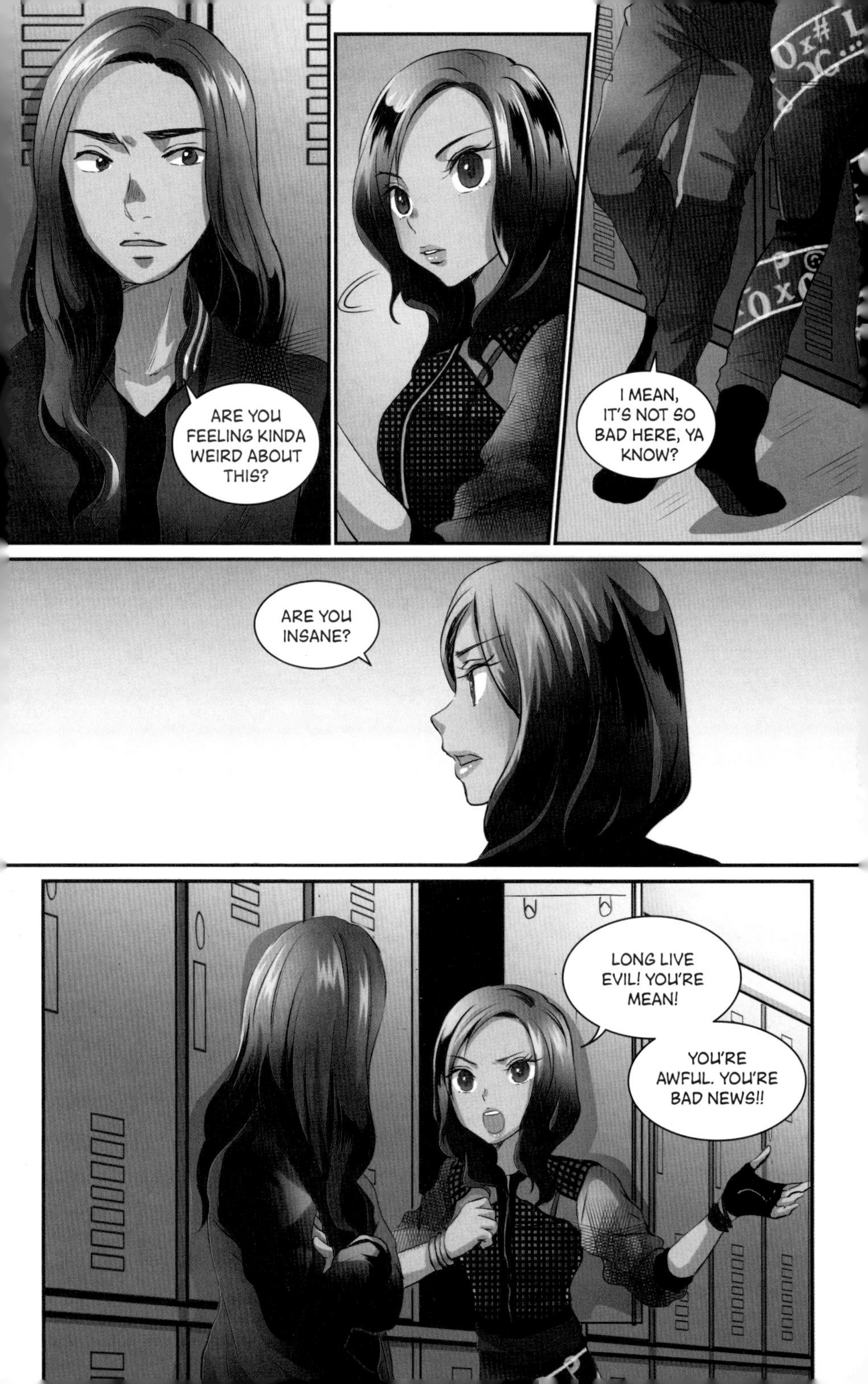
ARE YOU FEELING KINDA WEIRD ABOUT THIS?
I MEAN, IT'S NOT SO BAD HERE, YA KNOW?
ARE YOU INSANE?
LONG LIVE EVIL! YOU'RE MEAN!
YOU'RE AWFUL. YOU'RE BAD NEWS!!

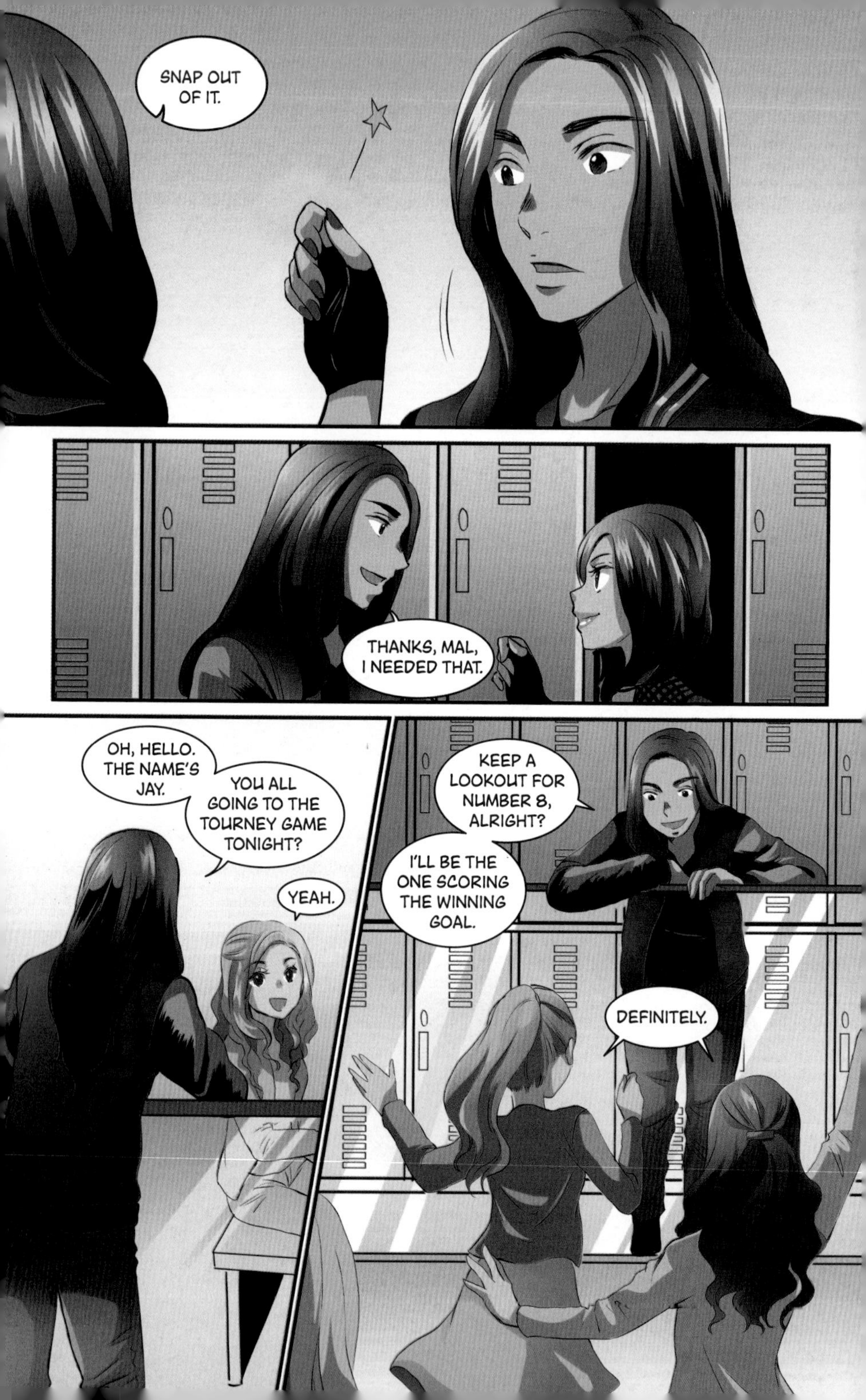
SNAP OUT OF IT.
THANKS, MAL, I NEEDED THAT.
OH, HELLO. THE NAME'S JAY.
YOU ALL GOING TO THE TOURNEY GAME TONIGHT?
YEAH.
KEEP A LOOKOUT FOR NUMBER 8, ALRIGHT?
I'LL BE THE ONE SCORING THE WINNING GOAL.
DEFINITELY.

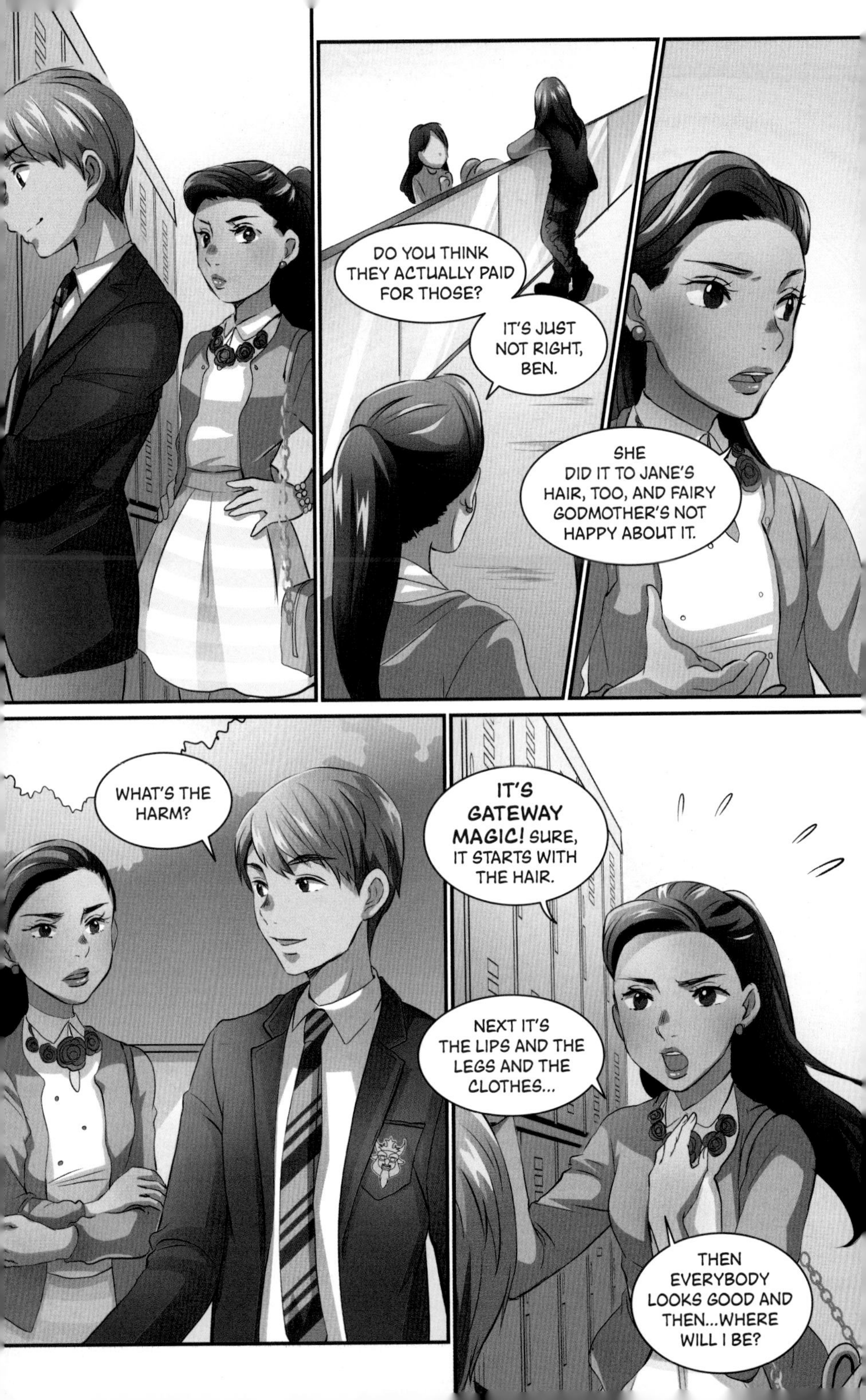
DO YOU THINK THEY ACTUALLY PAID FOR THOSE?
IT'S JUST NOT RIGHT, BEN.
SHE DID IT TO JANE'S HAIR, TOO, AND FAIRY GODMOTHER'S NOT HAPPY ABOUT IT.
WHAT'S THE HARM?
IT'S GATEWAY MAGIC! SURE, IT STARTS WITH THE HAIR.
NEXT IT'S THE LIPS AND THE LEGS AND THE CLOTHES...
THEN EVERYBODY LOOKS GOOD AND THEN...WHERE WILL I BE?

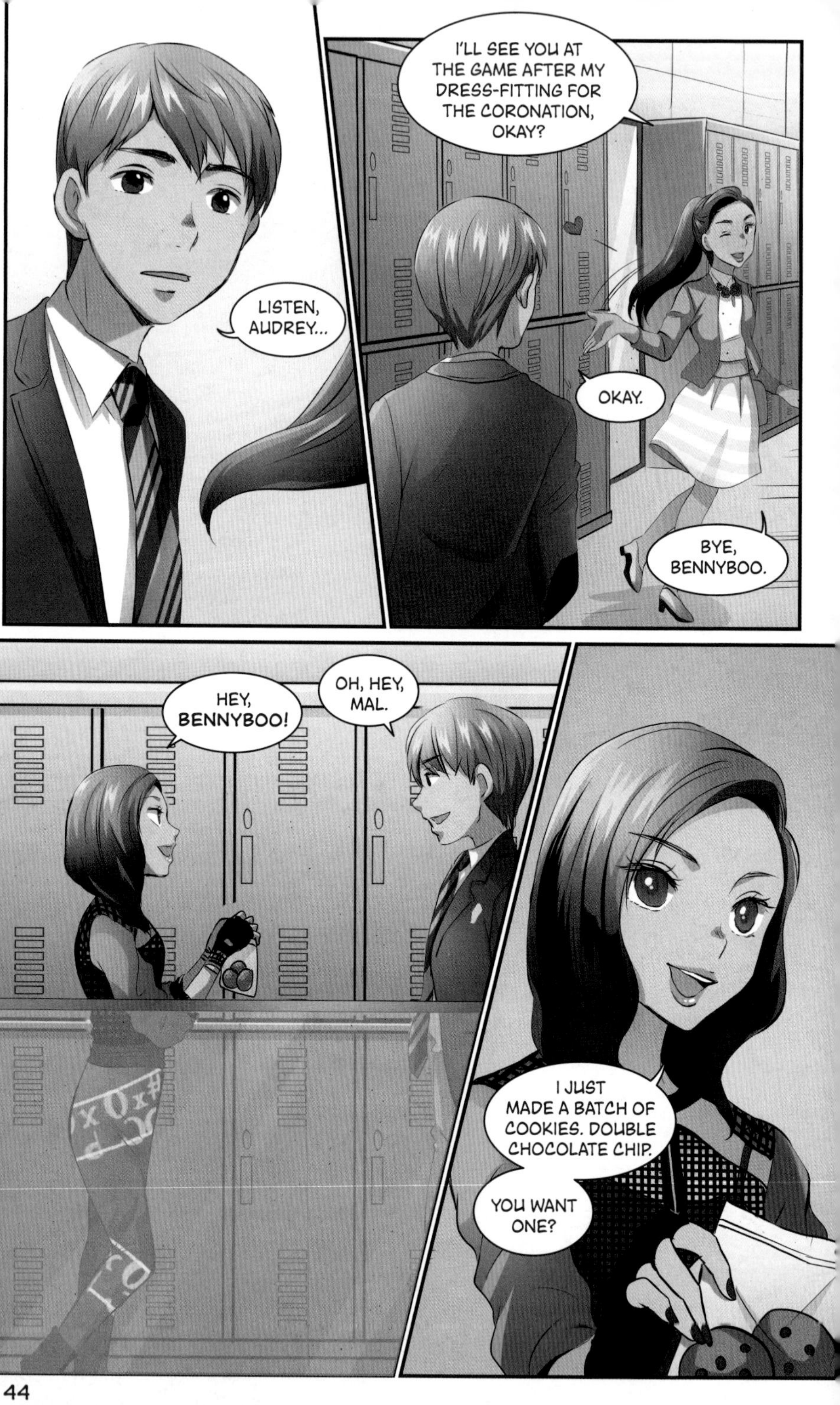
LISTEN, AUDREY...
I'LL SEE YOU AT THE GAME AFTER MY DRESS-FITTING FOR THE CORONATION, OKAY?
OKAY.
BYE, BENNYBOO.
HEY, BENNYBOO!
OH, HEY, MAL.
I JUST MADE A BATCH OF COOKIES. DOUBLE CHOCOLATE CHIP.
YOU WANT ONE?

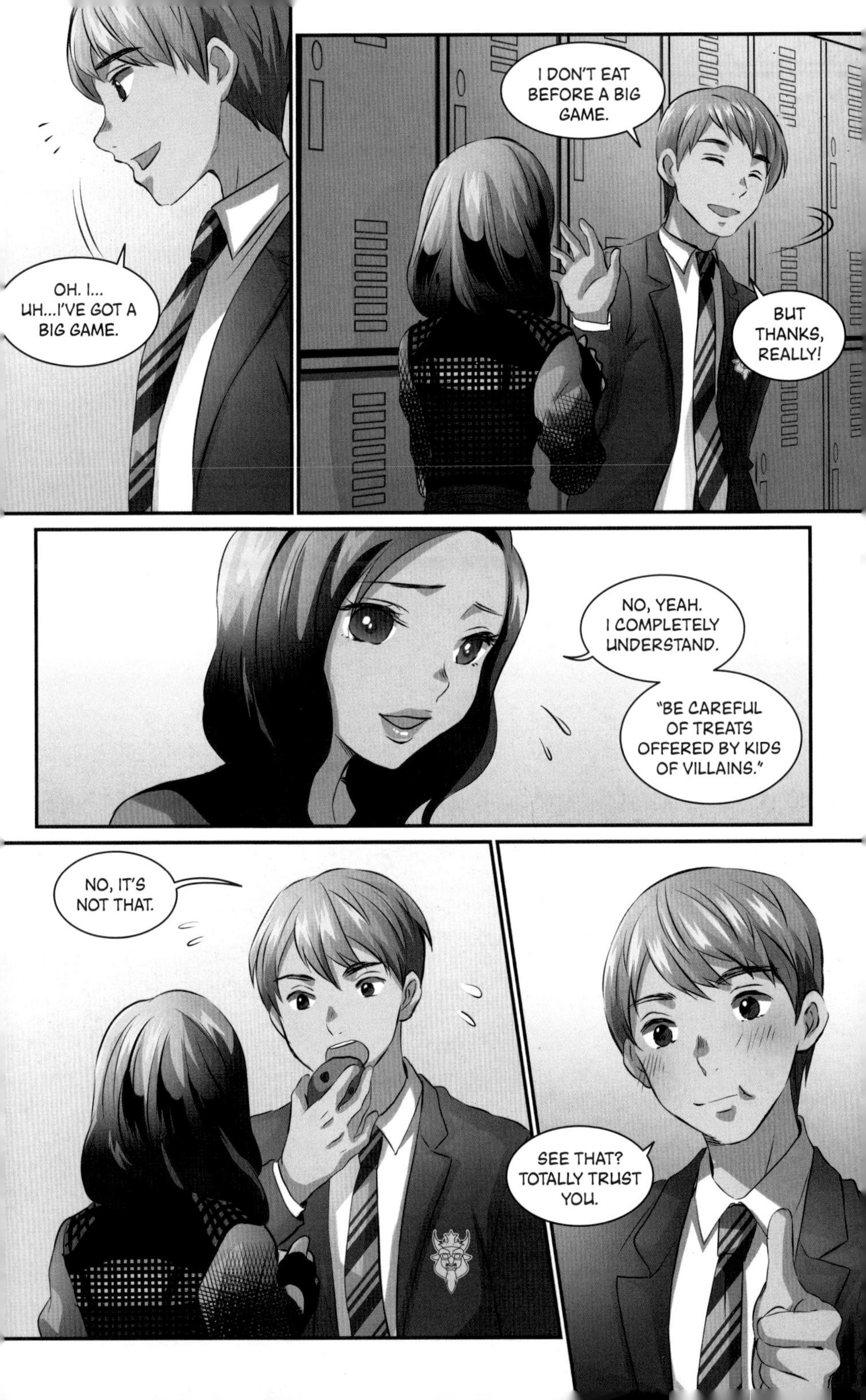
OH. I... UH...I'VE GOT A BIG GAME.
I DON'T EAT BEFORE A BIG GAME.
BUT THANKS, REALLY!
NO, YEAH. I COMPLETELY UNDERSTAND.
"BE CAREFUL OF TREATS OFFERED BY KIDS OF VILLAINS."
NO, IT'S NOT THAT.
SEE THAT? TOTALLY TRUST YOU.

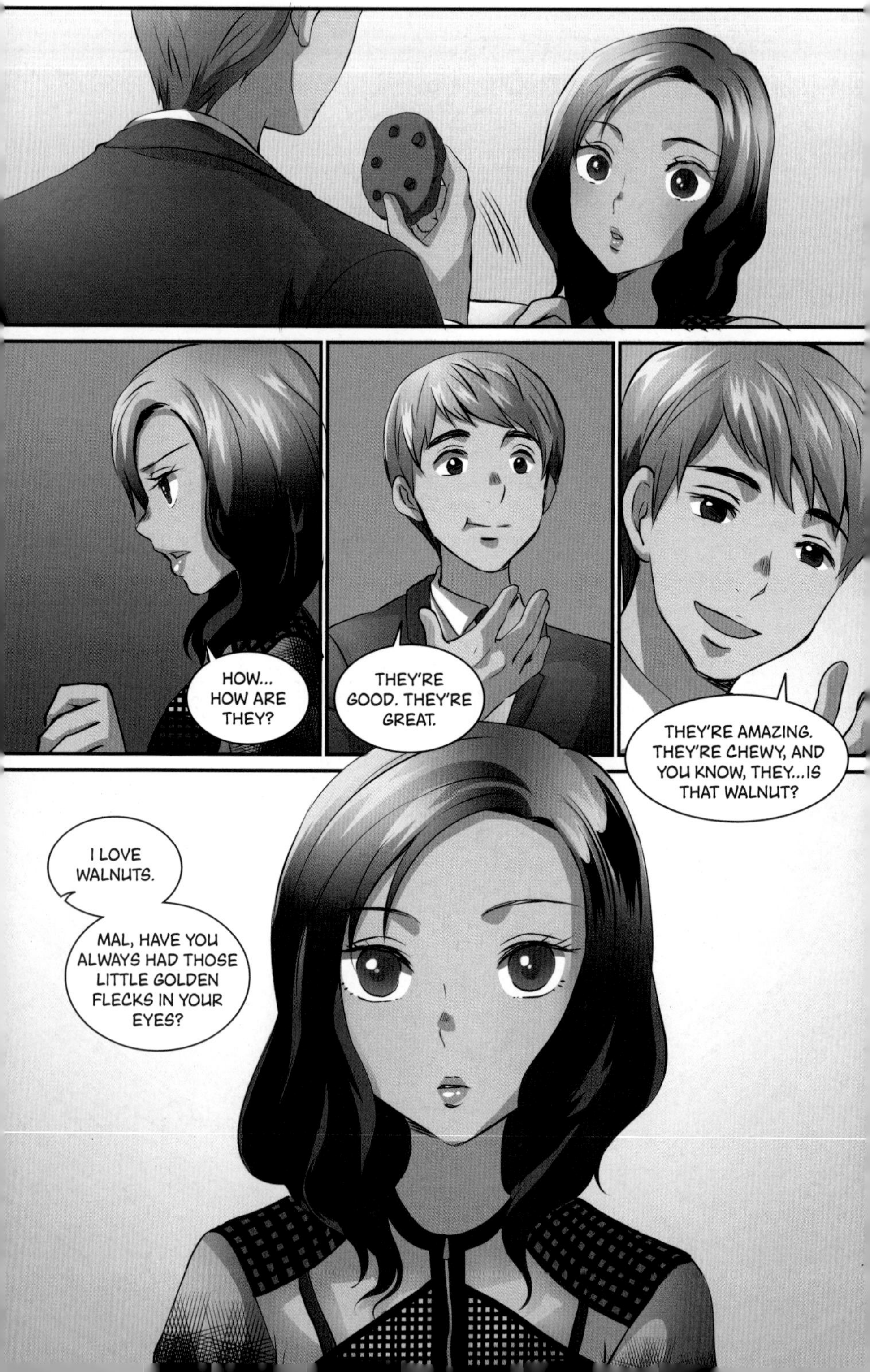
HOW... HOW ARE THEY?
THEY'RE GOOD. THEY'RE GREAT.
THEY'RE AMAZING. THEY'RE CHEWY, AND YOU KNOW, THEY...IS THAT WALNUT?
I LOVE WALNUTS.
MAL, HAVE YOU ALWAYS HAD THOSE LITTLE GOLDEN FLECKS IN YOUR EYES?

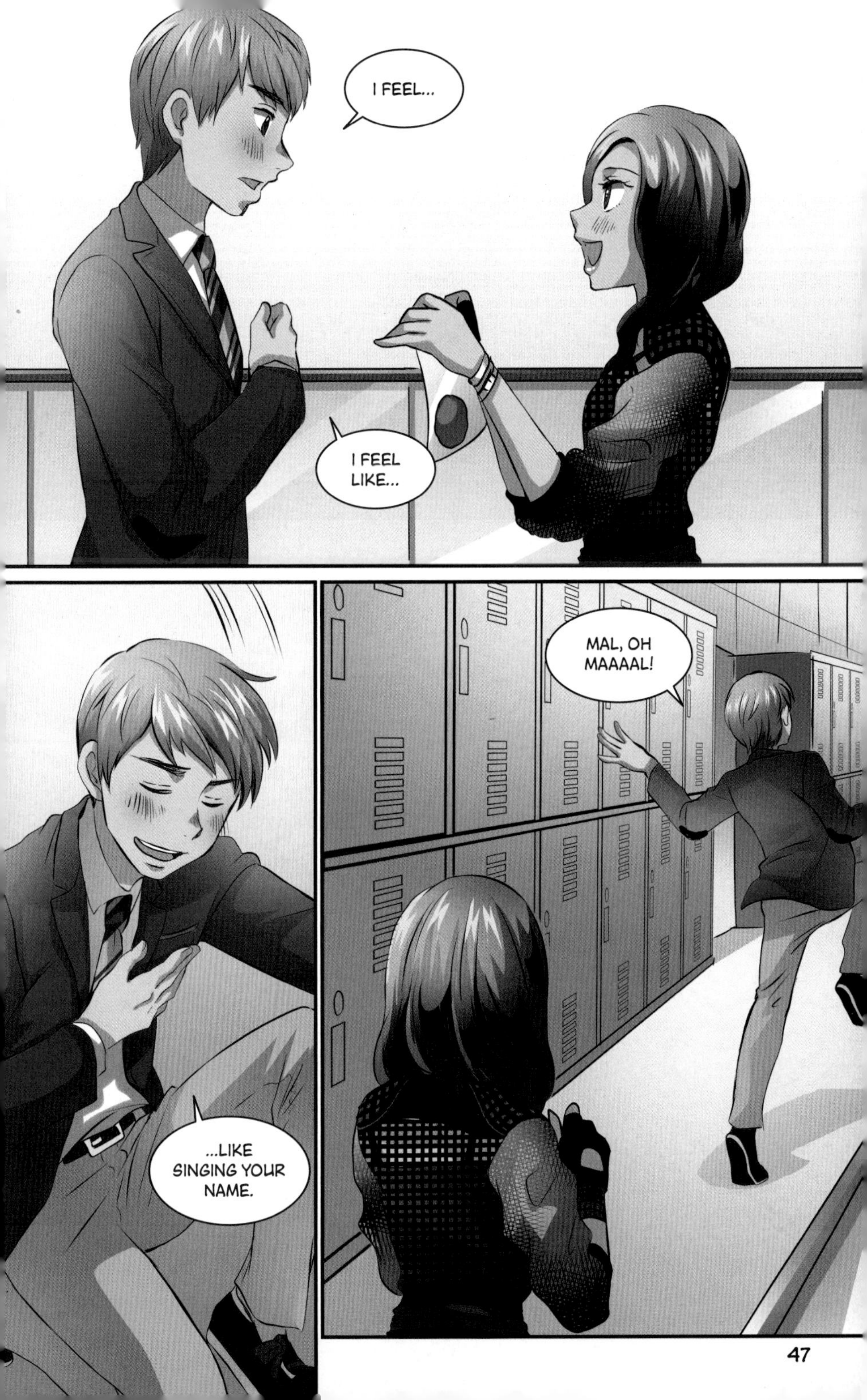
I FEEL...
I FEEL LIKE...
...LIKE SINGING YOUR NAME.
MAL, OH MAAAAL!

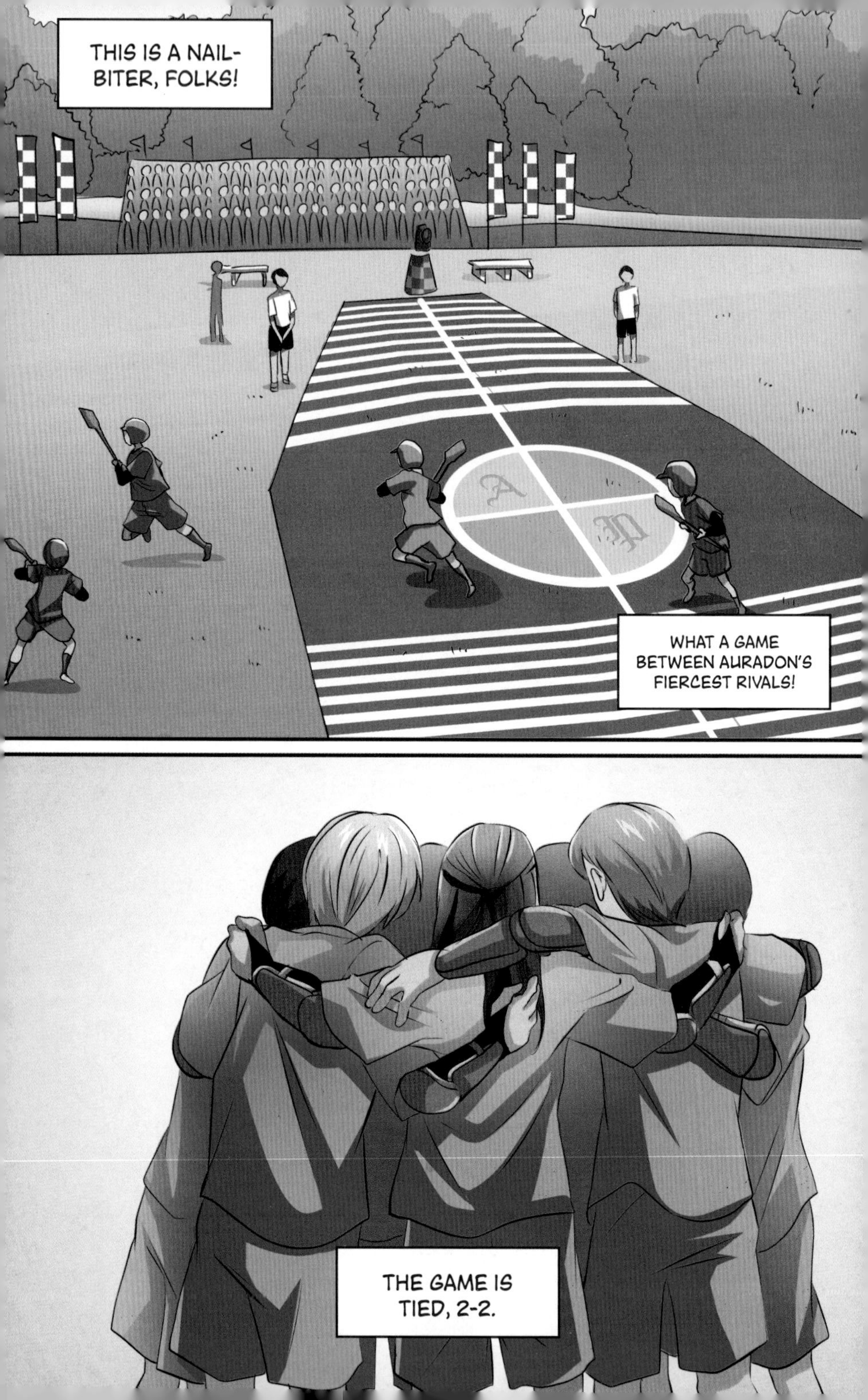
THIS IS A NAIL-BITER, FOLKS!
WHAT A GAME BETWEEN AURADON'S FIERCEST RIVALS!
THE GAME IS TIED, 2-2.

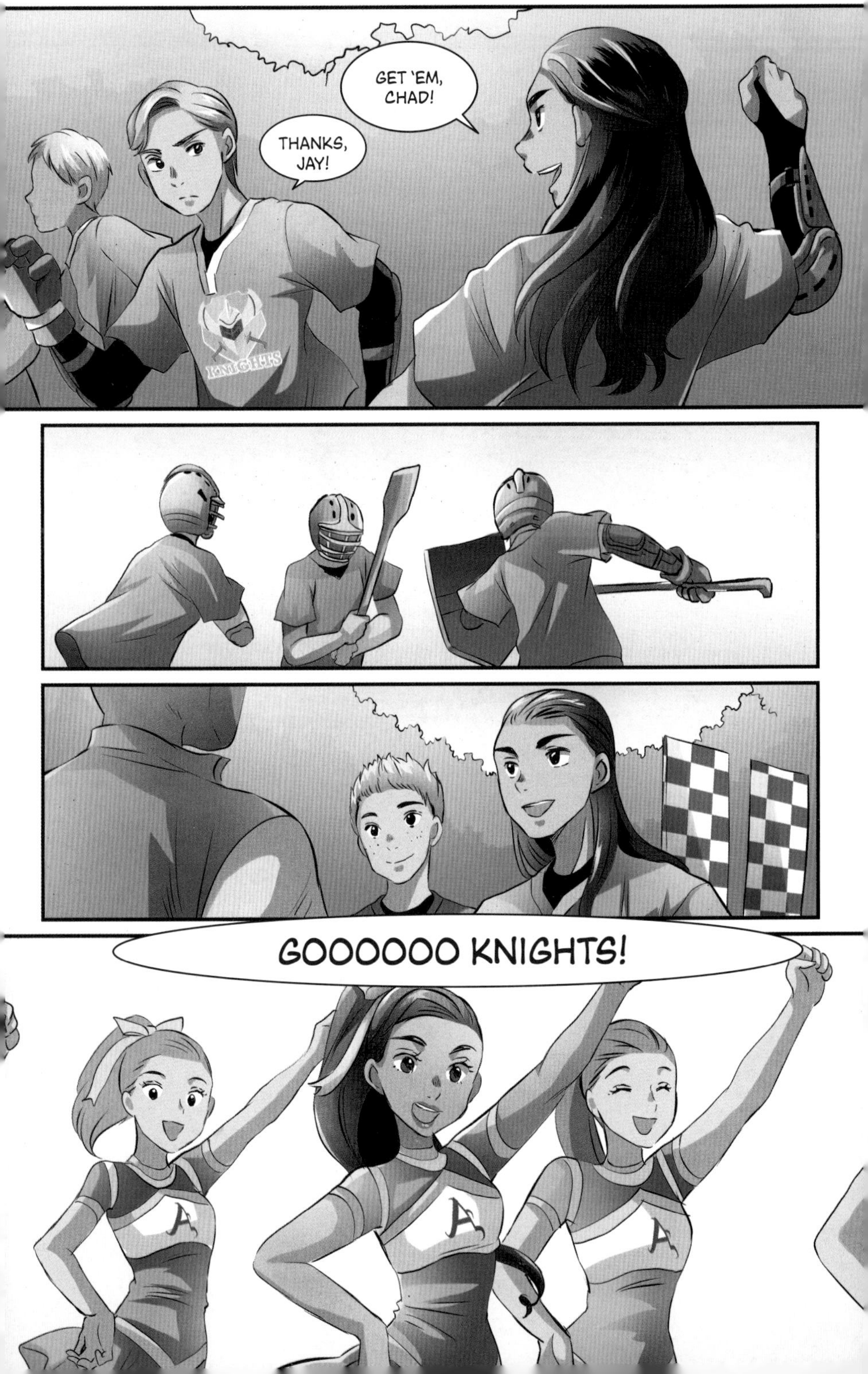
GET 'EM, CHAD!
THANKS, JAY!
KNIGHTS
GOOOOOO KNIGHTS!

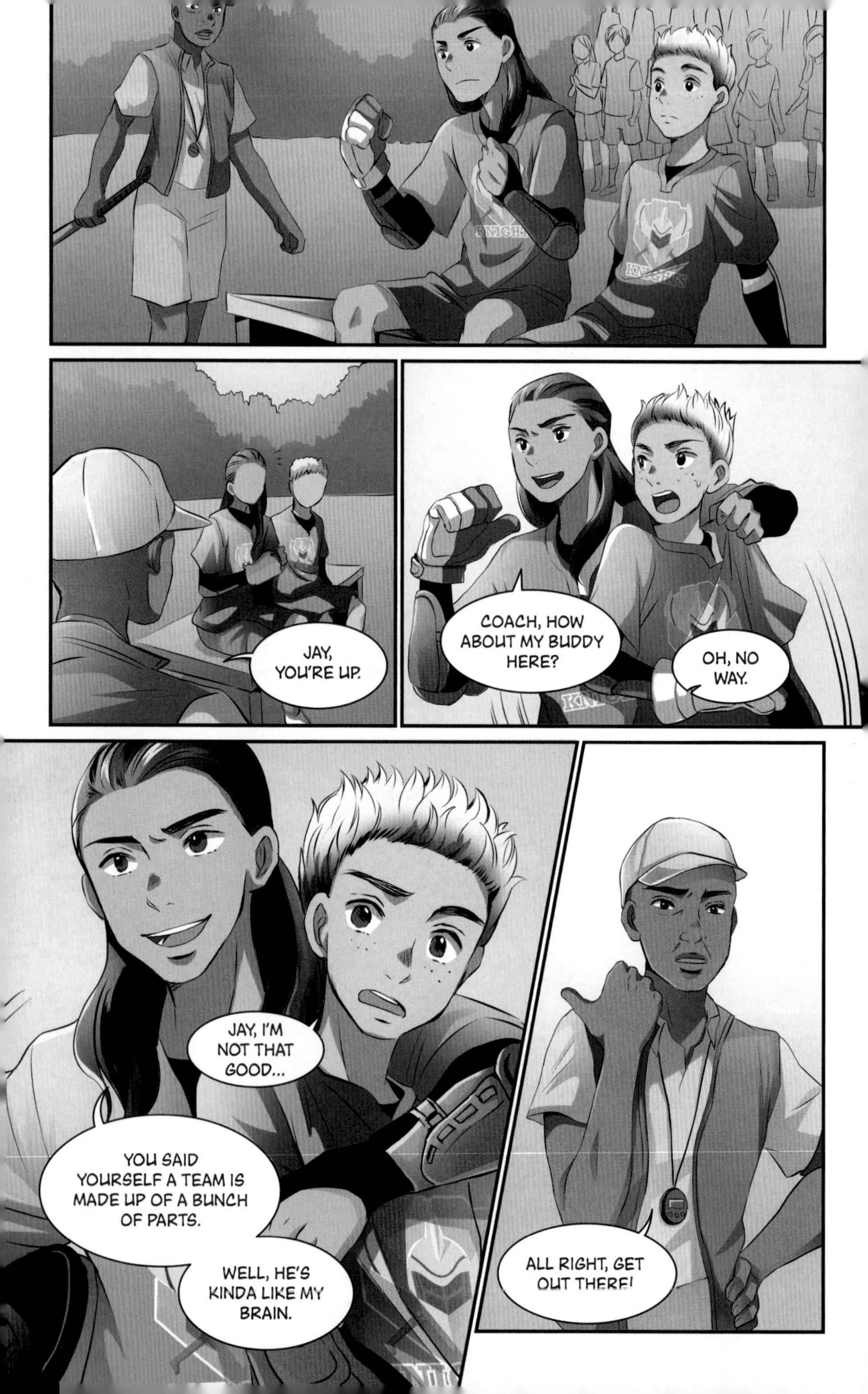
JAY, YOU'RE UP.
COACH, HOW ABOUT MY BUDDY HERE?
OH, NO WAY.
JAY, I'M NOT THAT GOOD...
YOU SAID YOURSELF A TEAM IS MADE UP OF A BUNCH OF PARTS.
WELL, HE'S KINDA LIKE MY BRAIN.
ALL RIGHT, GET OUT THERE!

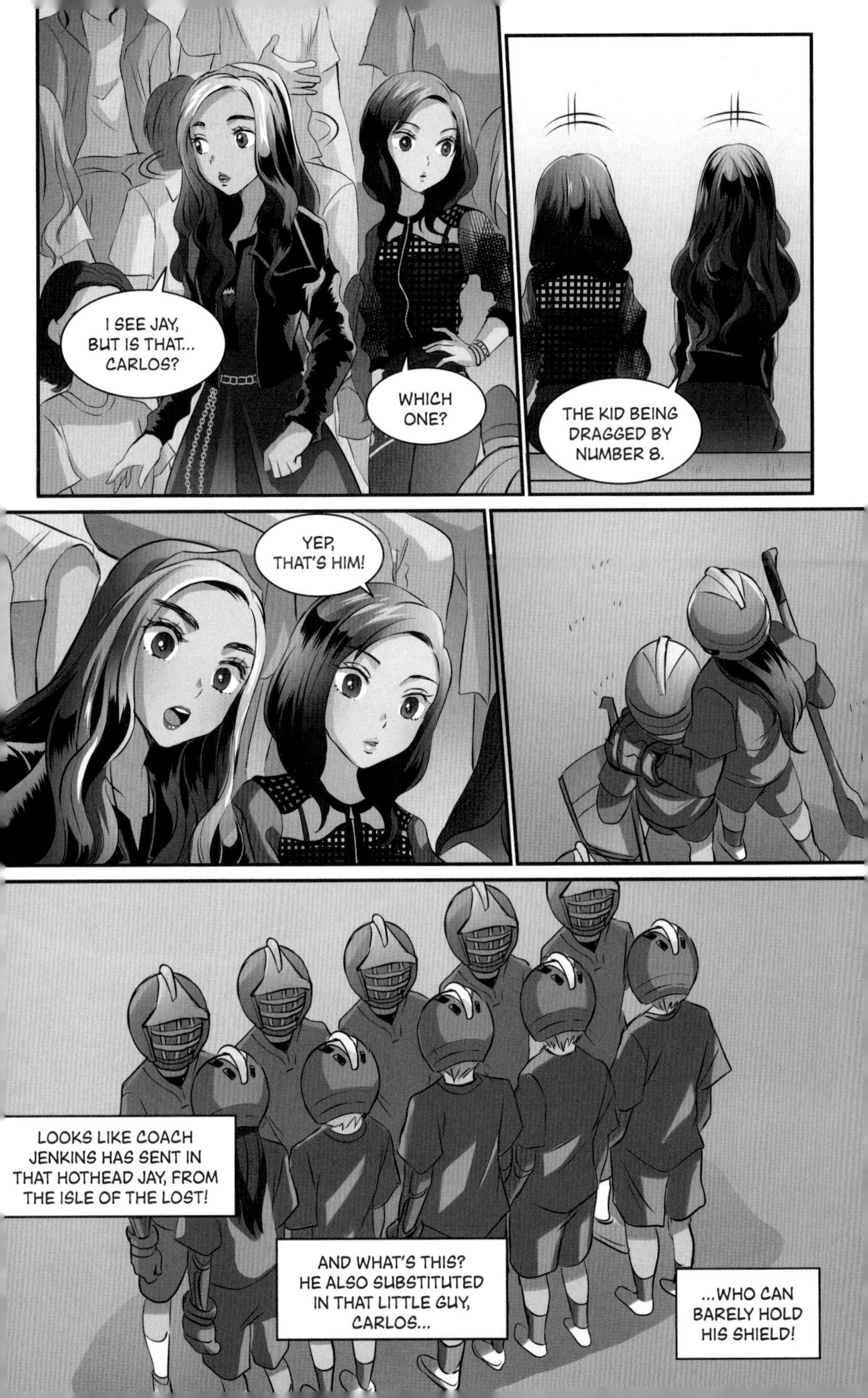
I SEE JAY, BUT IS THAT... CARLOS?
WHICH ONE?
THE KID BEING DRAGGED BY NUMBER 8.
YEP, THAT'S HIM!
LOOKS LIKE COACH JENKINS HAS SENT IN THAT HOTHEAD JAY, FROM THE ISLE OF THE LOST!
AND WHAT'S THIS? HE ALSO SUBSTITUTED IN THAT LITTLE GUY, CARLOS...
...WHO CAN BARELY HOLD HIS SHIELD!

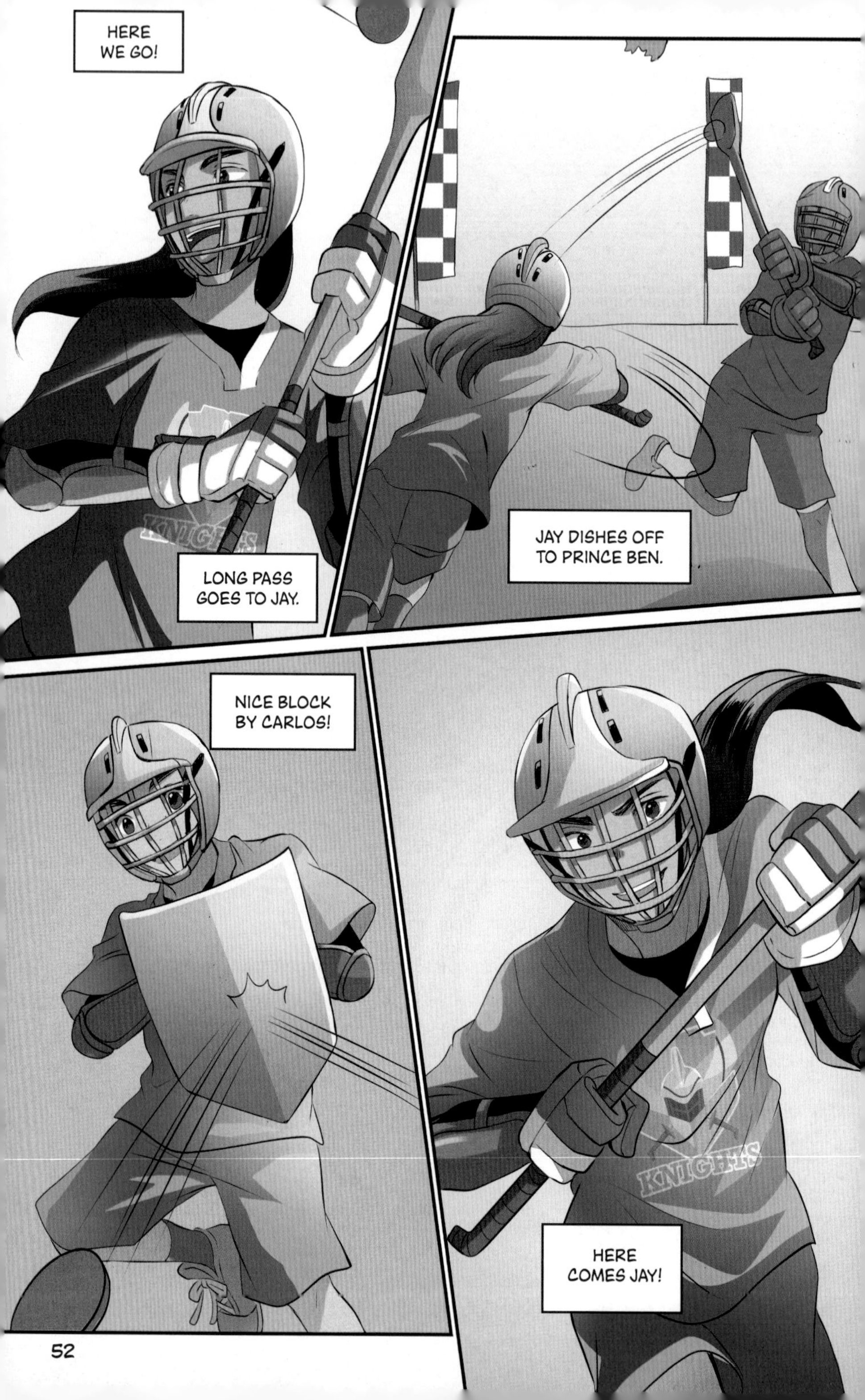
HERE WE GO!
LONG PASS GOES TO JAY.
KNIGHTS
JAY DISHES OFF TO PRINCE BEN.
NICE BLOCK BY CARLOS!
KNIGHTS
HERE COMES JAY!

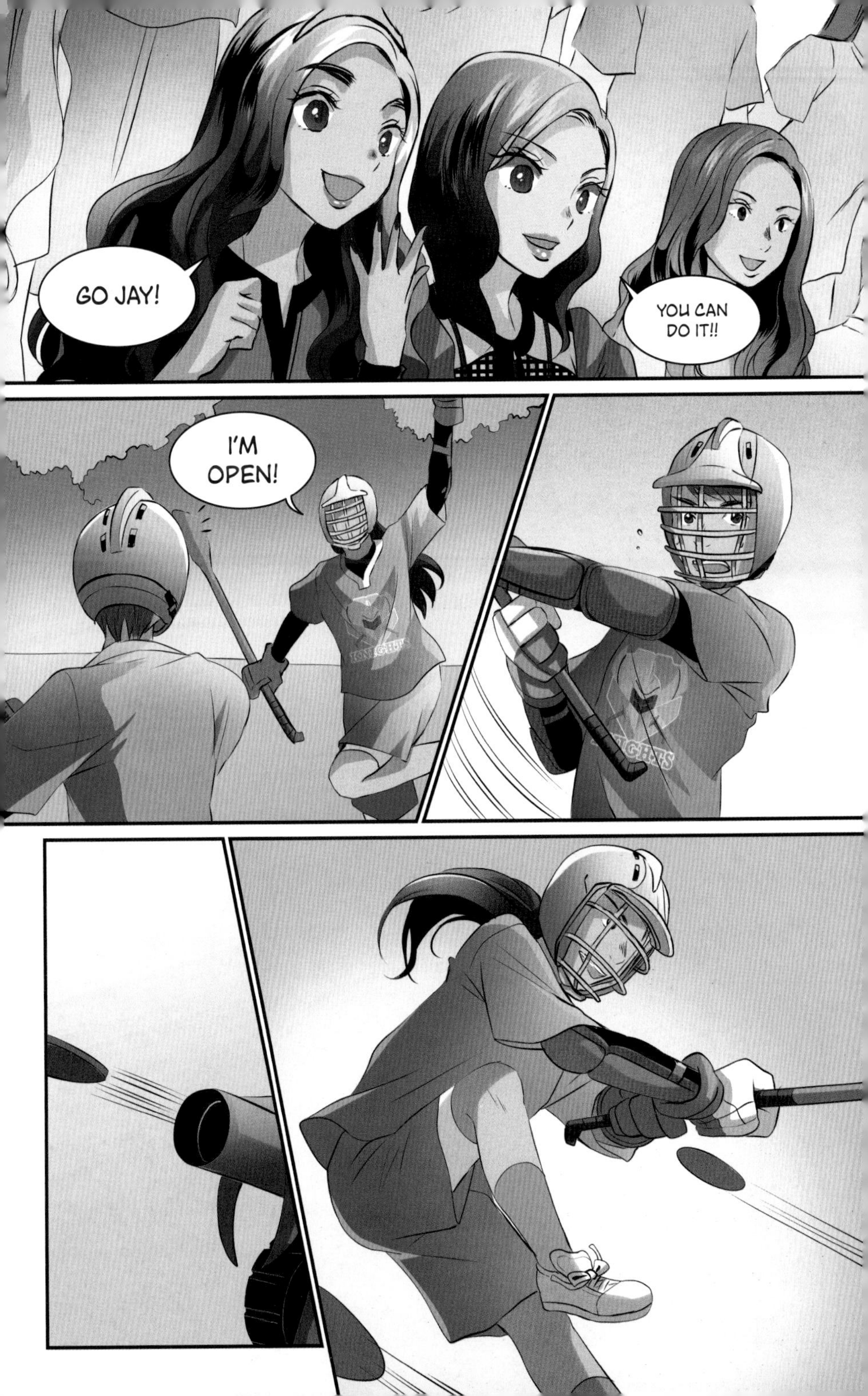
GO JAY!
YOU CAN DO IT!!
I'M OPEN!

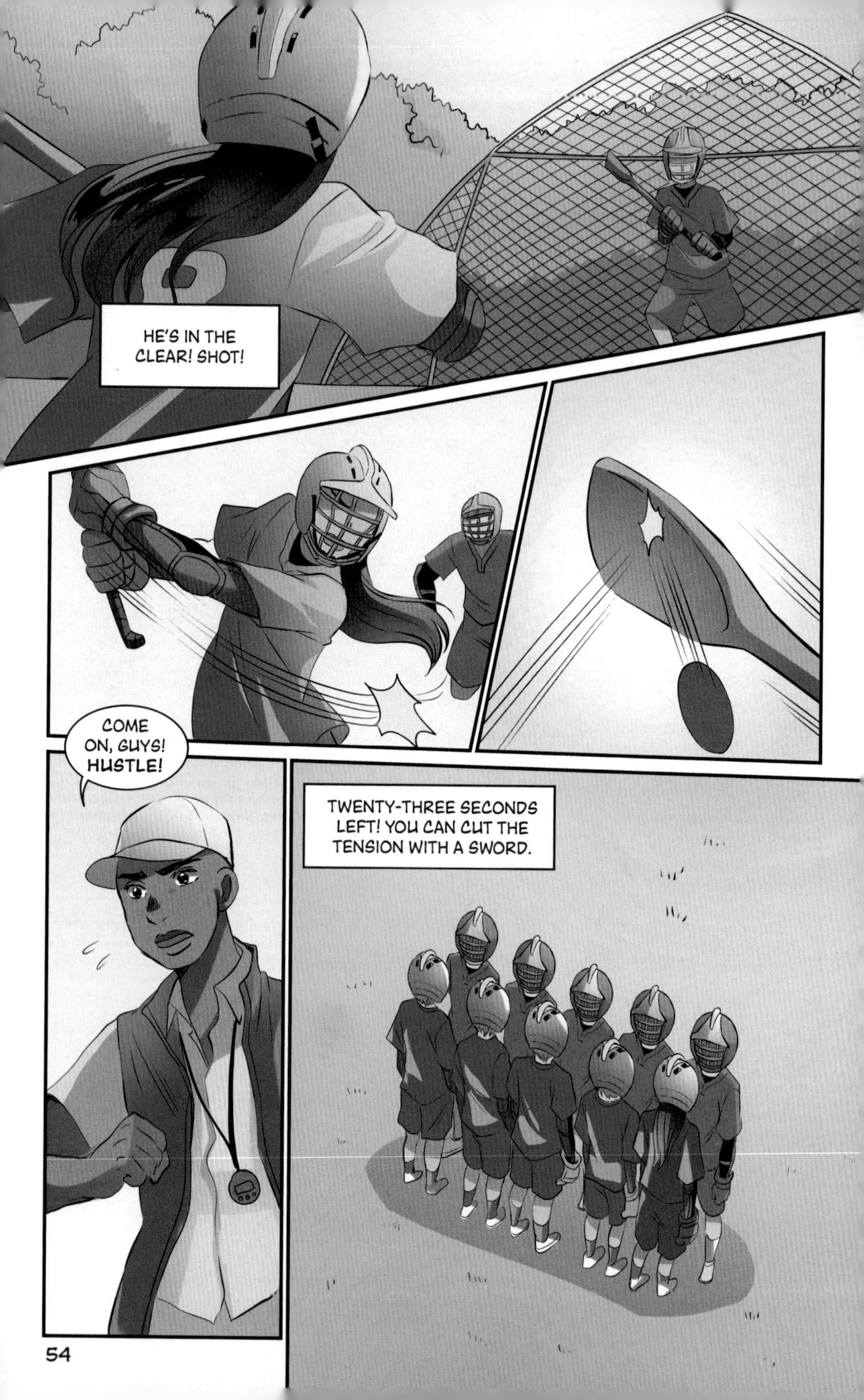
HE'S IN THE CLEAR! SHOT!
COME ON, GUYS! HUSTLE!
TWENTY-THREE SECONDS LEFT! YOU CAN CUT THE TENSION WITH A SWORD.

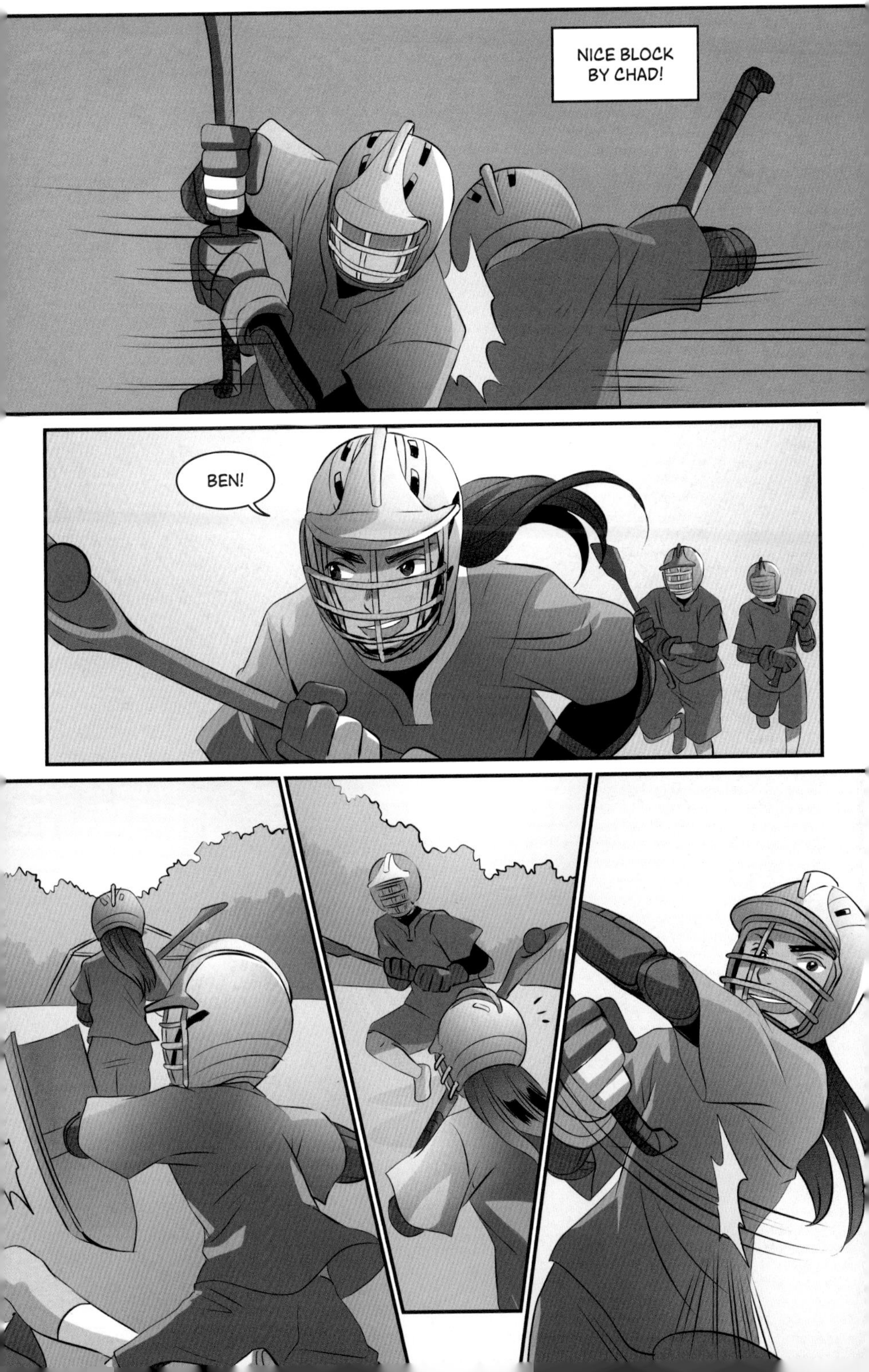
NICE BLOCK BY CHAD!
BEN!

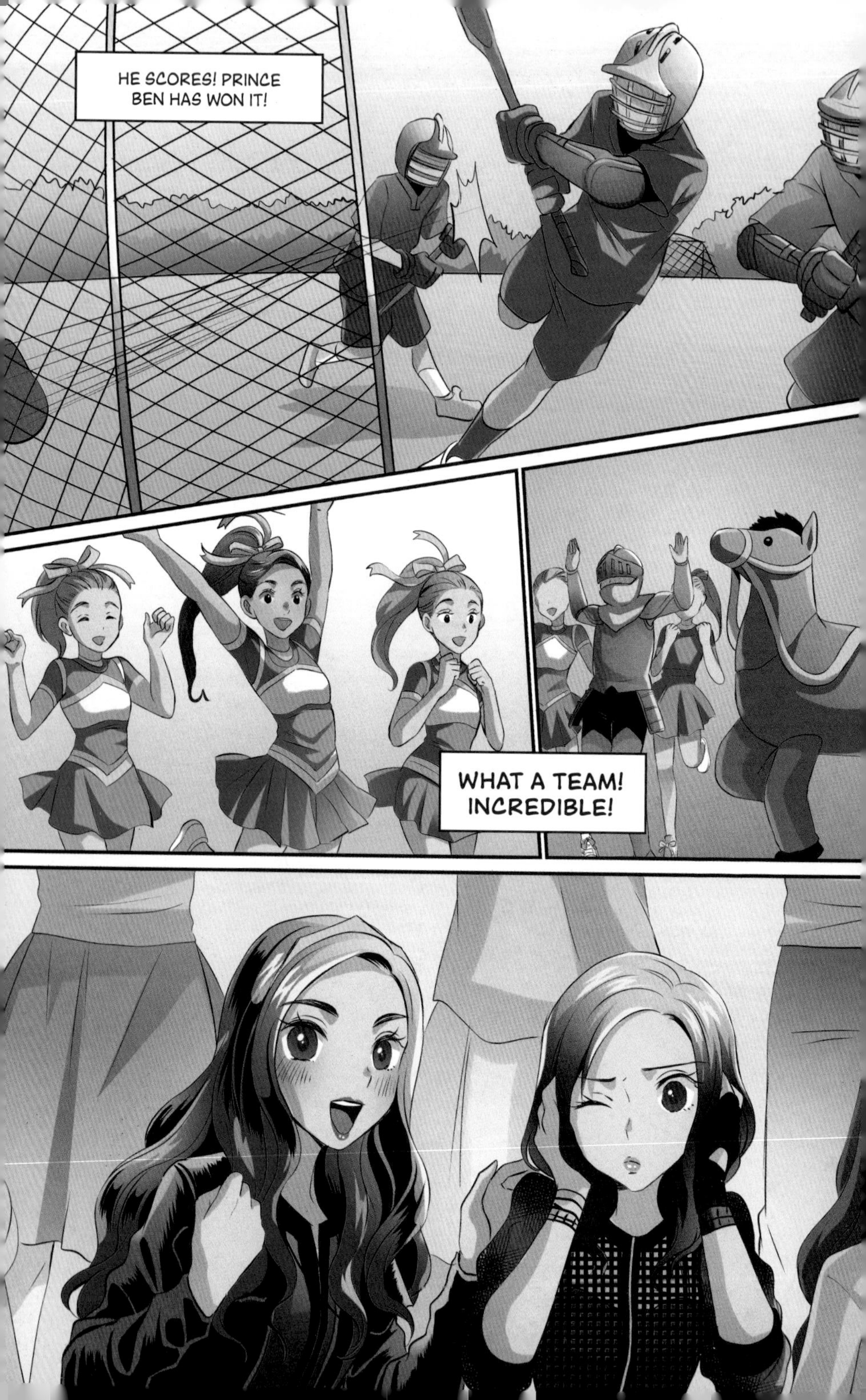
HE SCORES! PRINCE BEN HAS WON IT!
WHAT A TEAM! INCREDIBLE!

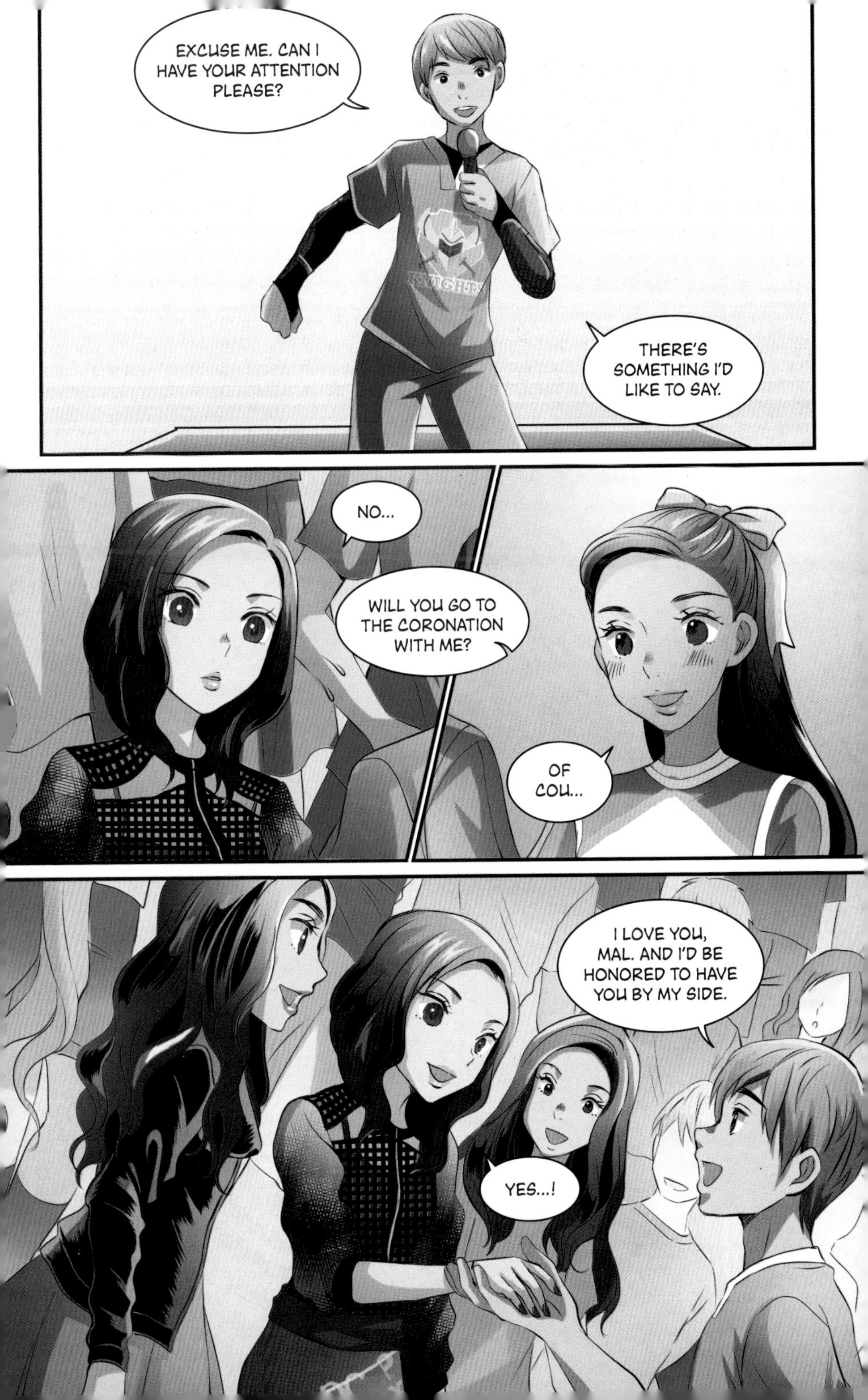
EXCUSE ME. CAN I HAVE YOUR ATTENTION PLEASE?
THERE'S SOMETHING I'D LIKE TO SAY.
NO...
WILL YOU GO TO THE CORONATION WITH ME?
OF COU...
I LOVE YOU, MAL. AND I'D BE HONORED TO HAVE YOU BY MY SIDE.
YES...!

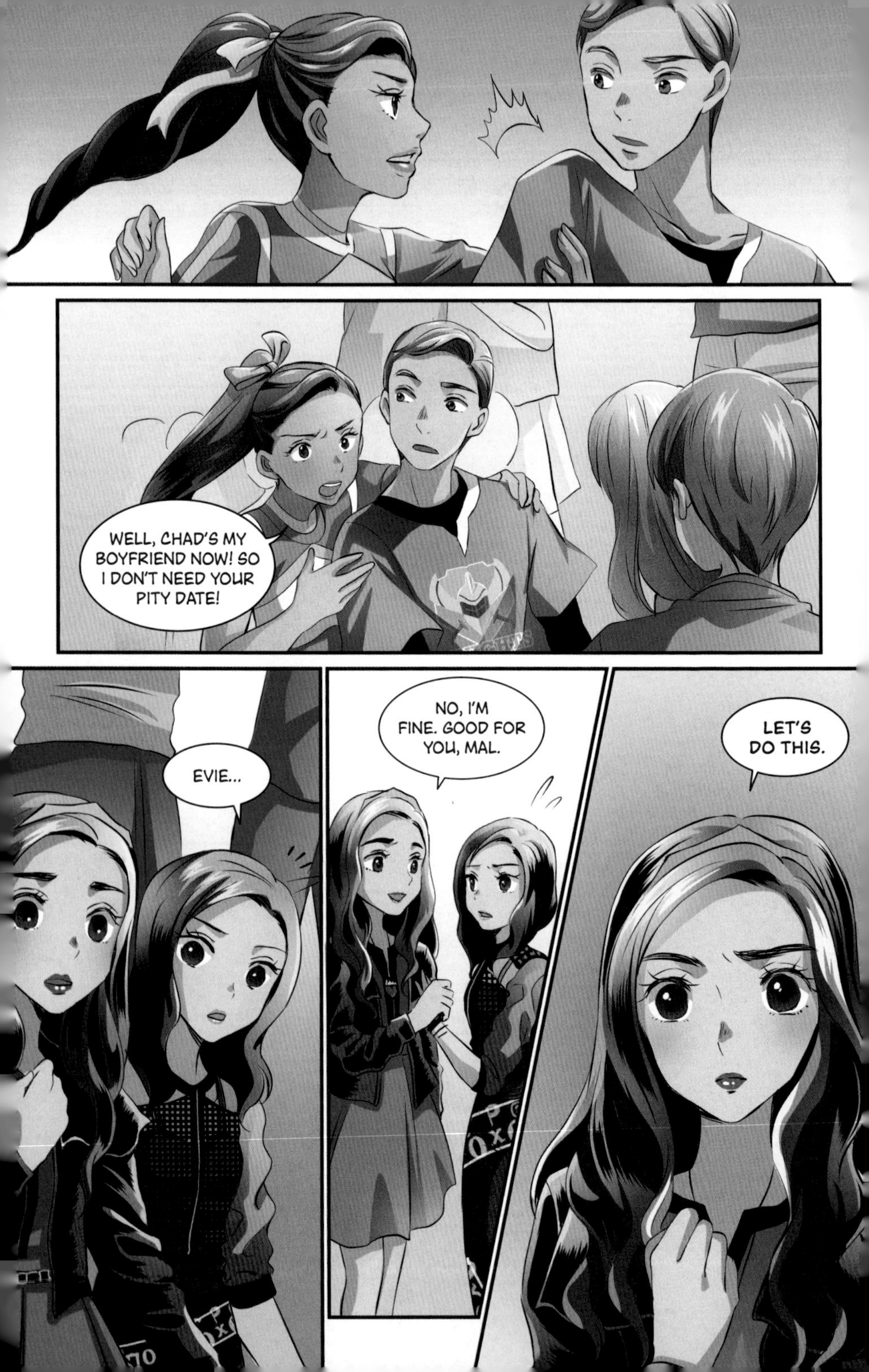
WELL, CHAD'S MY BOYFRIEND NOW! SO I DON'T NEED YOUR PITY DATE!
EVIE...
NO, I'M FINE. GOOD FOR YOU, MAL.
LET'S DO THIS.

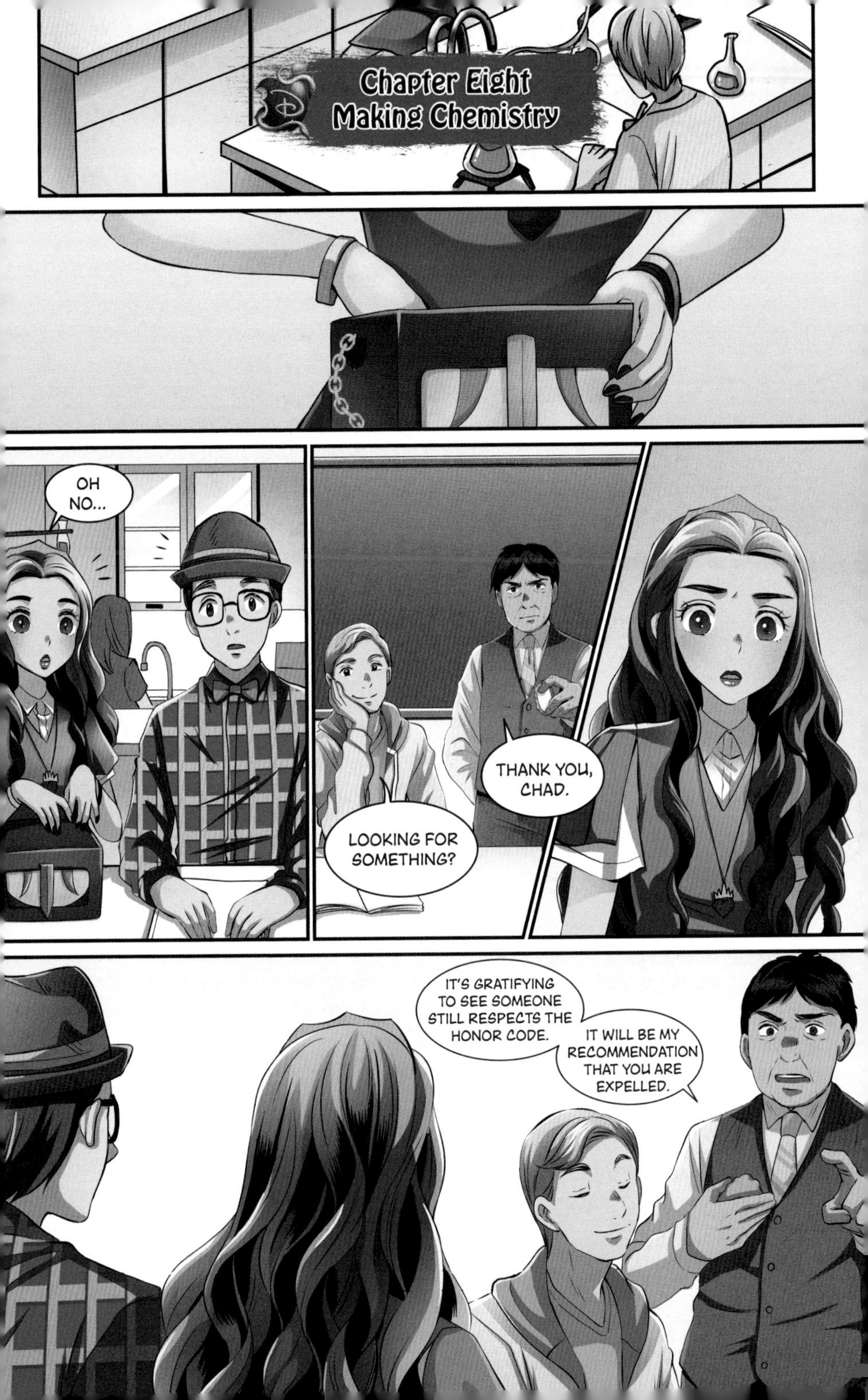
Chapter Eight
Making Chemistry
OH NO...
LOOKING FOR SOMETHING?
THANK YOU, CHAD.
IT'S GRATIFYING TO SEE SOMEONE STILL RESPECTS THE HONOR CODE.
IT WILL BE MY RECOMMENDATION THAT YOU ARE EXPELLED.

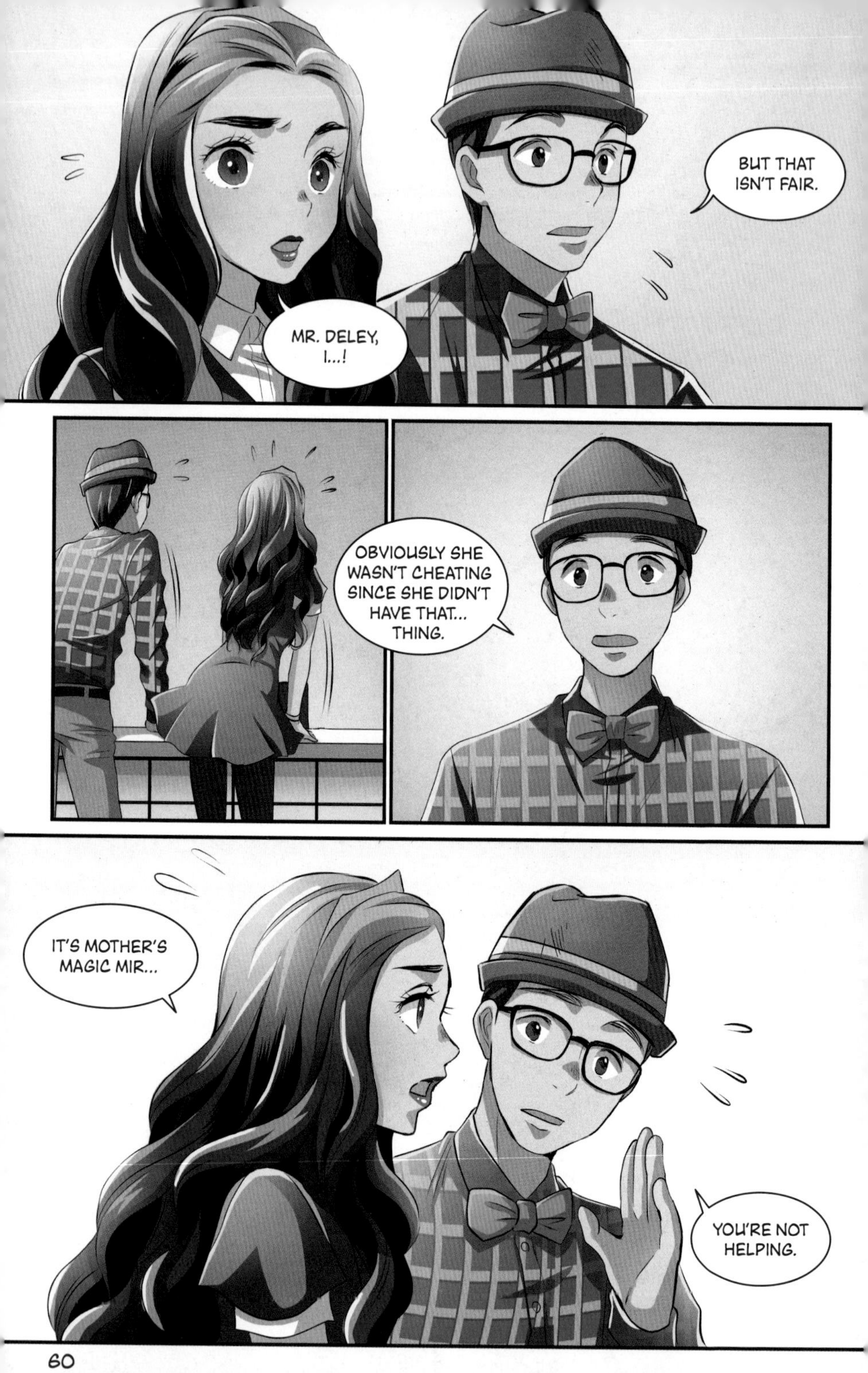
MR. DELEY, I...!
BUT THAT ISN'T FAIR.
OBVIOUSLY SHE WASN'T CHEATING SINCE SHE DIDN'T HAVE THAT... THING.
IT'S MOTHER'S MAGIC MIR...
YOU'RE NOT HELPING.

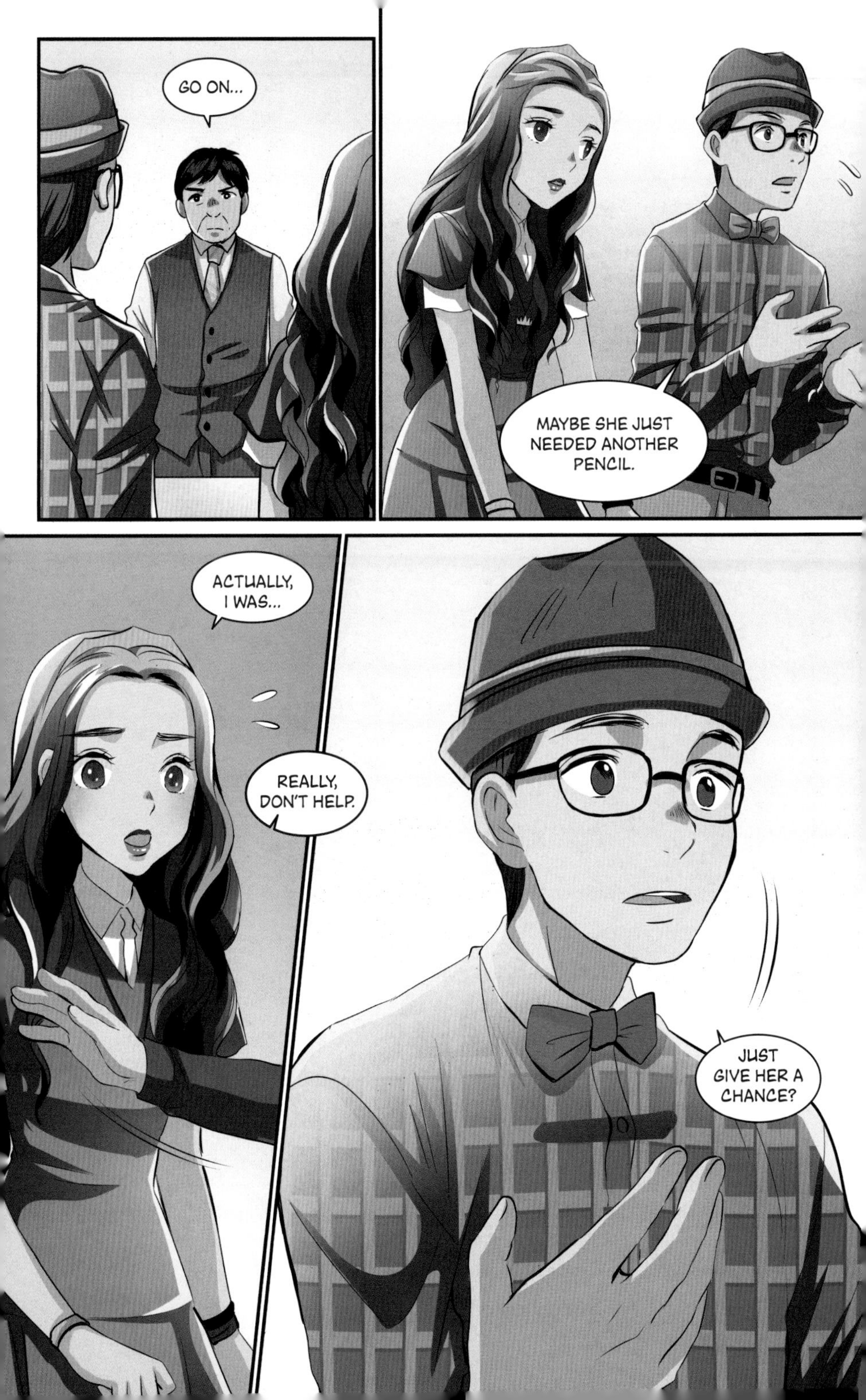
GO ON...
MAYBE SHE JUST NEEDED ANOTHER PENCIL.
ACTUALLY, I WAS...
REALLY, DON'T HELP.
JUST GIVE HER A CHANCE?

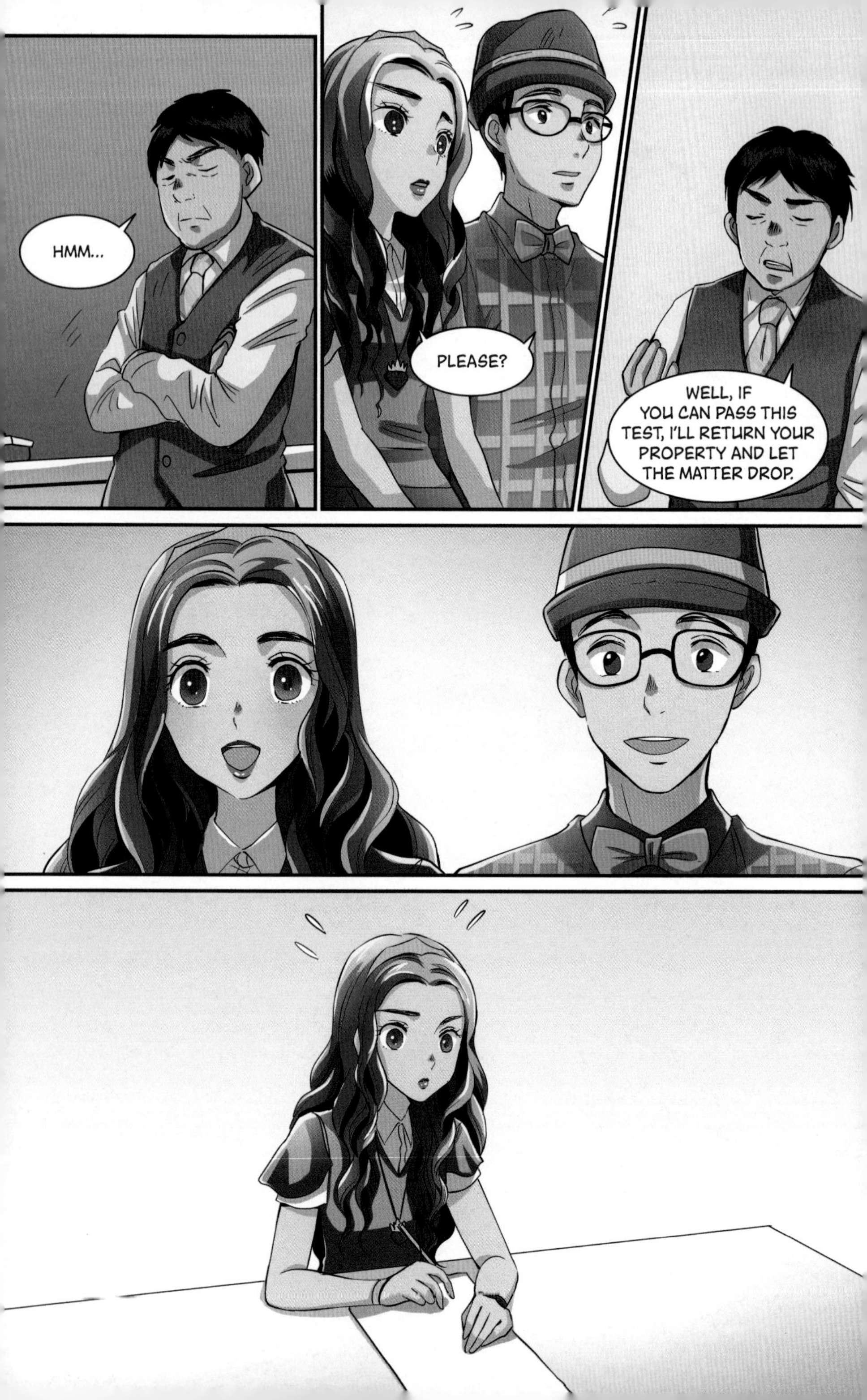
HMM...
PLEASE?
WELL, IF YOU CAN PASS THIS TEST, I'LL RETURN YOUR PROPERTY AND LET THE MATTER DROP.

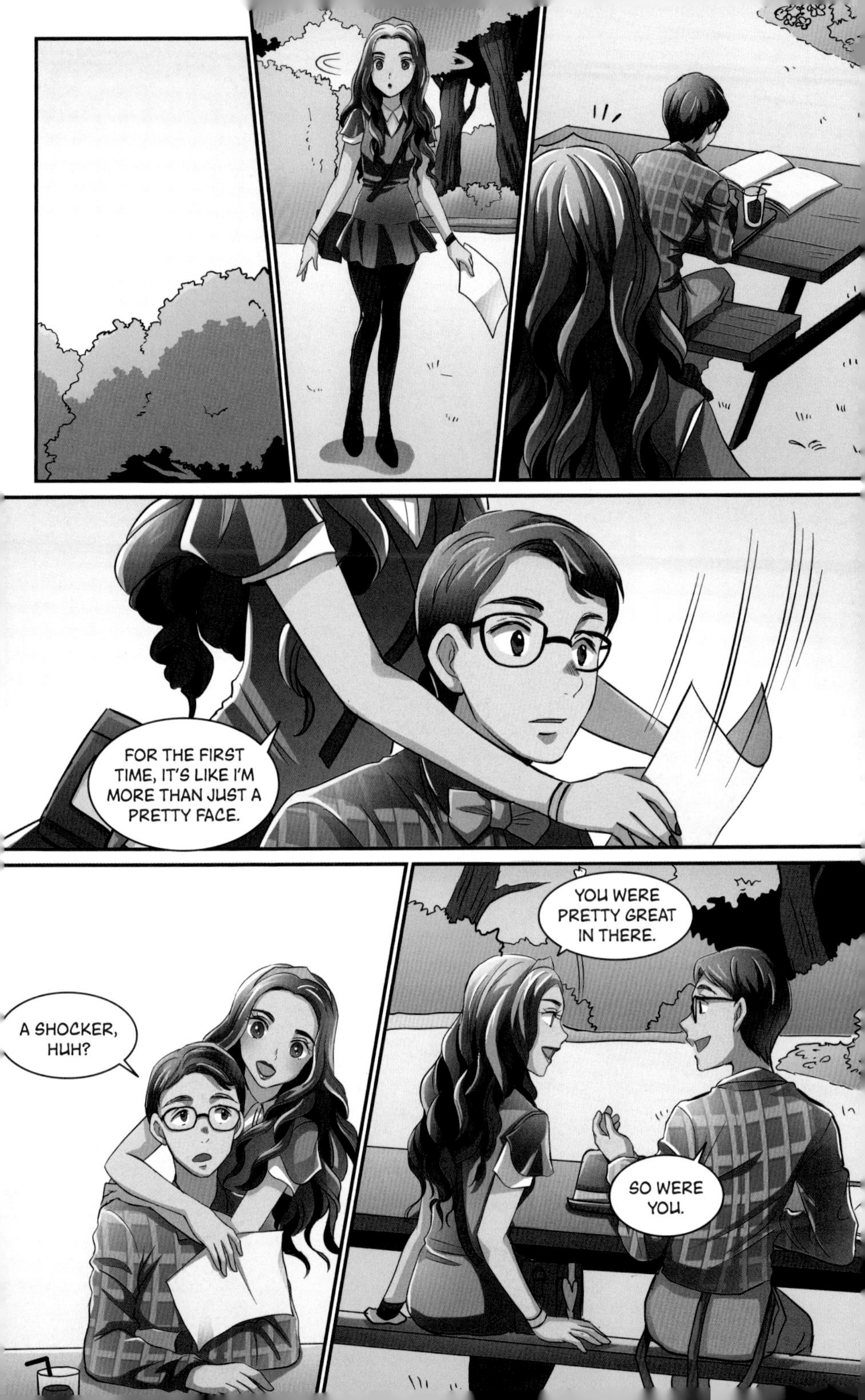
FOR THE FIRST TIME, IT'S LIKE I'M MORE THAN JUST A PRETTY FACE.
A SHOCKER, HUH?
YOU WERE PRETTY GREAT IN THERE.
SO WERE YOU.

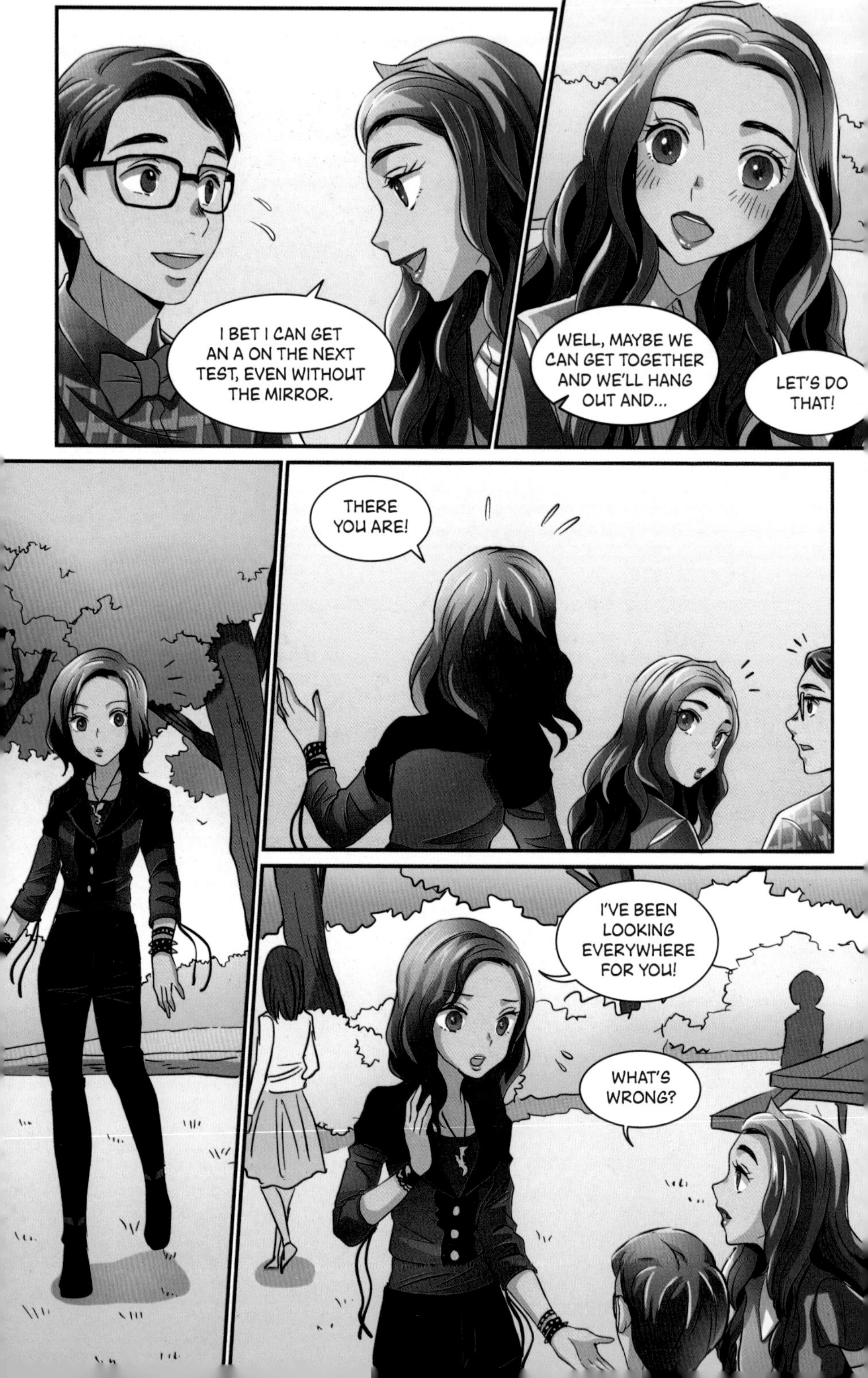
I BET I CAN GET AN A ON THE NEXT TEST, EVEN WITHOUT THE MIRROR.
WELL, MAYBE WE CAN GET TOGETHER AND WE'LL HANG OUT AND...
LET'S DO THAT!
THERE YOU ARE!
I'VE BEEN LOOKING EVERYWHERE FOR YOU!
WHAT'S WRONG?

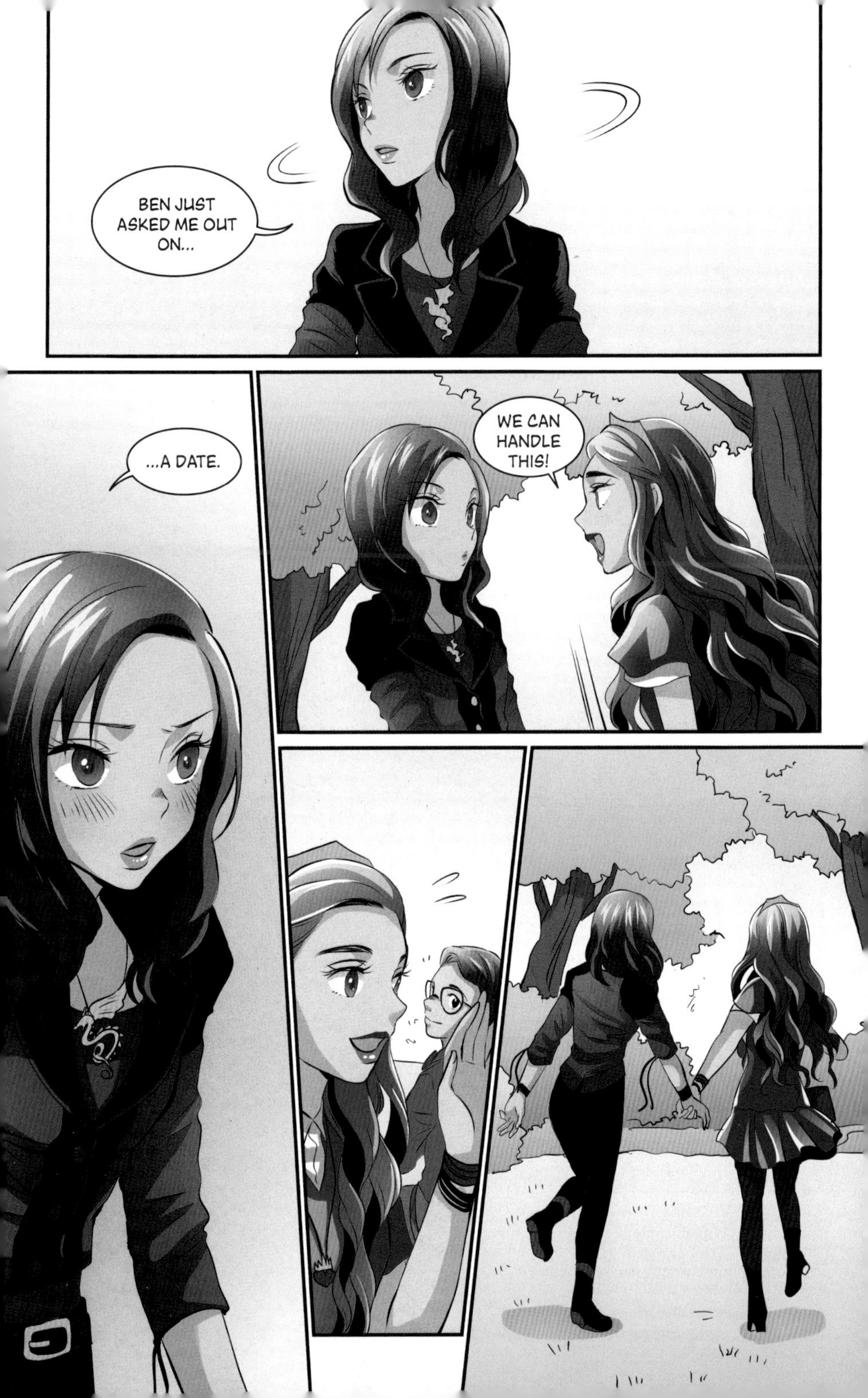
BEN JUST ASKED ME OUT ON...
...A DATE.
WE CAN HANDLE THIS!

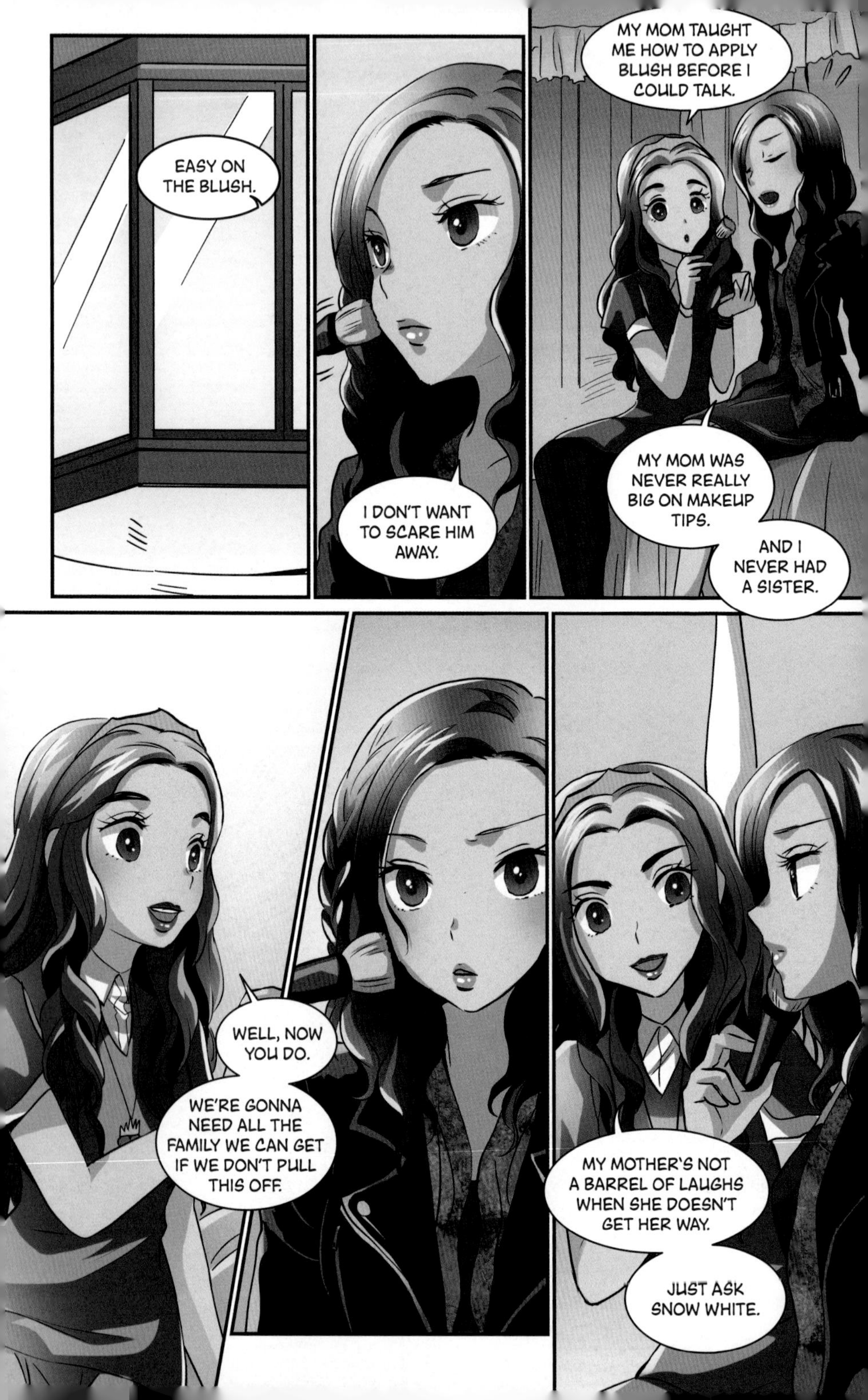
EASY ON THE BLUSH.
I DON'T WANT TO SCARE HIM AWAY.
MY MOM TAUGHT ME HOW TO APPLY BLUSH BEFORE I COULD TALK.
MY MOM WAS NEVER REALLY BIG ON MAKEUP TIPS.
AND I NEVER HAD A SISTER.
WELL, NOW YOU DO.
WE'RE GONNA NEED ALL THE FAMILY WE CAN GET IF WE DON'T PULL THIS OFF.
MY MOTHER'S NOT A BARREL OF LAUGHS WHEN SHE DOESN'T GET HER WAY.
JUST ASK SNOW WHITE.

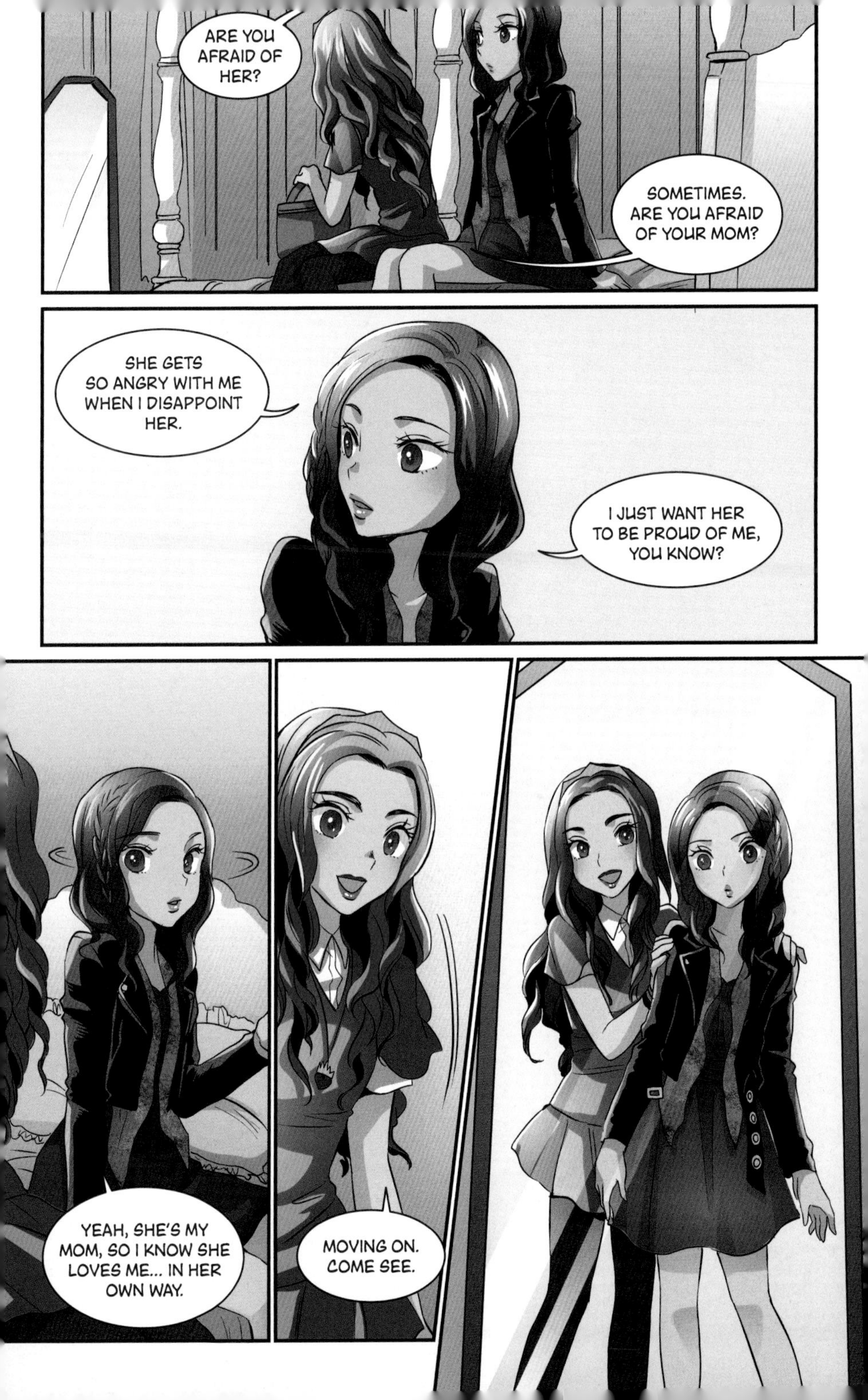
ARE YOU AFRAID OF HER?
SOMETIMES. ARE YOU AFRAID OF YOUR MOM?
SHE GETS SO ANGRY WITH ME WHEN I DISAPPOINT HER.
I JUST WANT HER TO BE PROUD OF ME, YOU KNOW?
YEAH, SHE'S MY MOM, SO I KNOW SHE LOVES ME... IN HER OWN WAY.
MOVING ON. COME SEE.

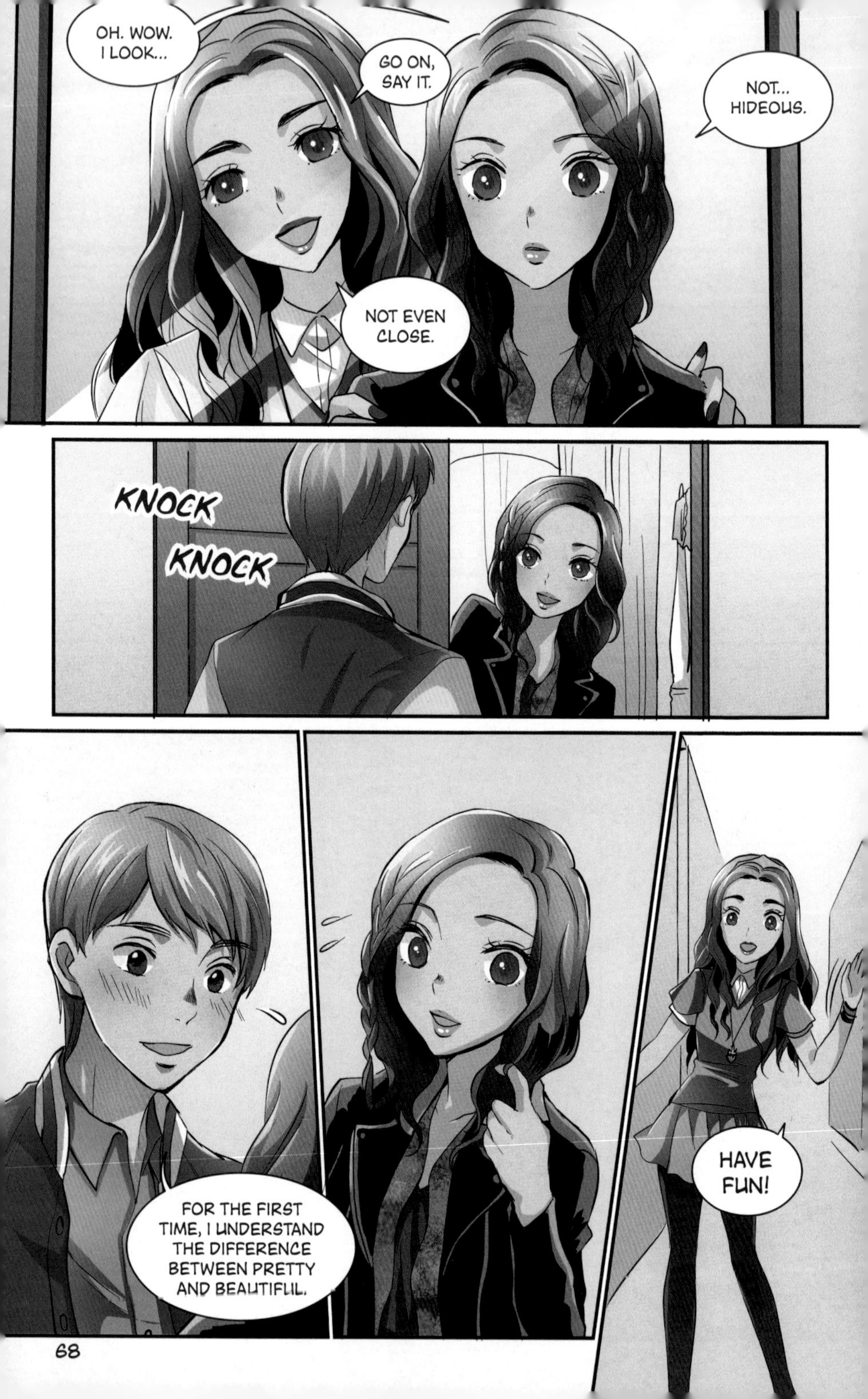
OH. WOW. I LOOK...
GO ON, SAY IT.
NOT... HIDEOUS.
NOT EVEN CLOSE.
KNOCK
KNOCK
FOR THE FIRST TIME, I UNDERSTAND THE DIFFERENCE BETWEEN PRETTY AND BEAUTIFUL.
HAVE FUN!

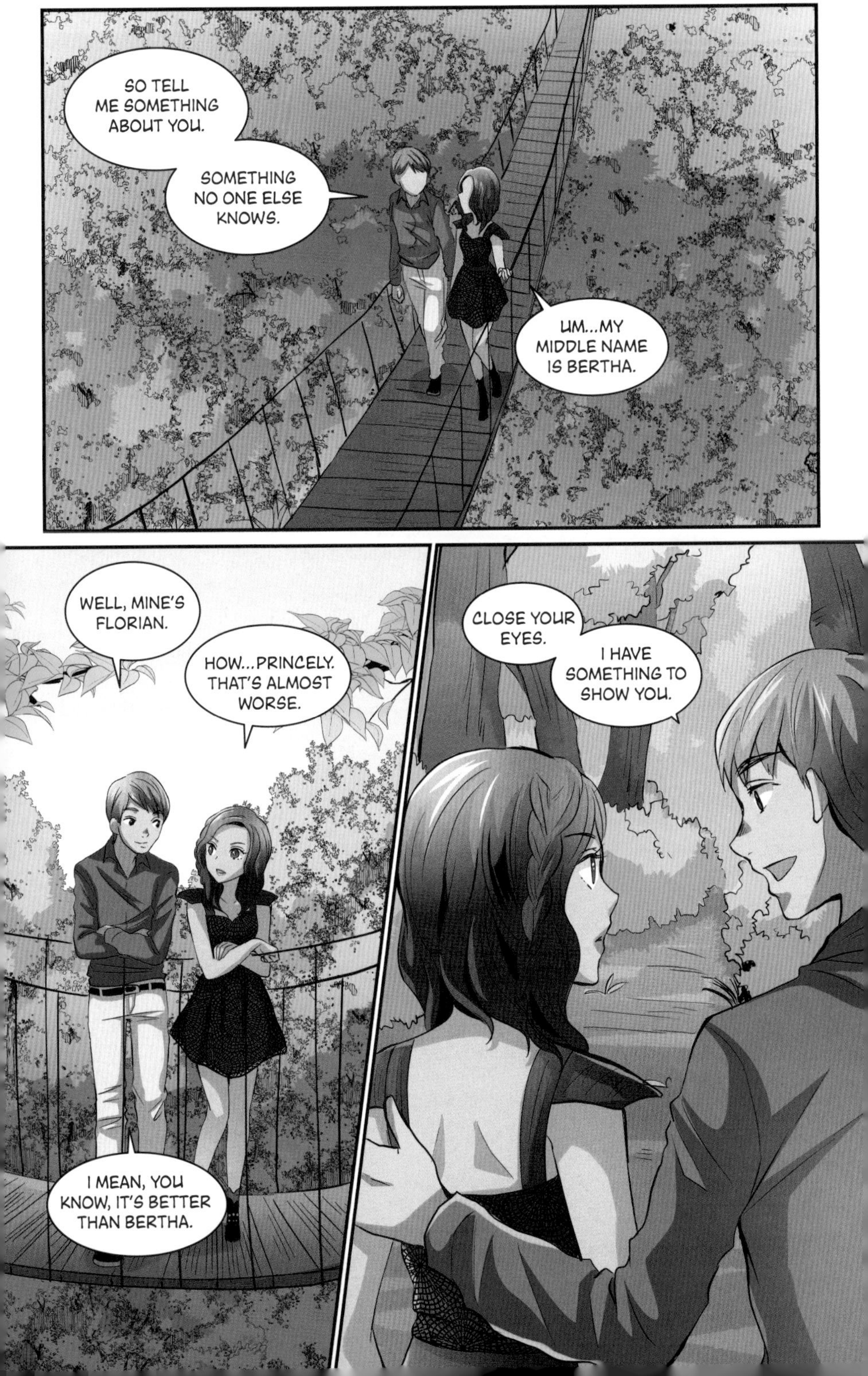
SO TELL ME SOMETHING ABOUT YOU.
SOMETHING NO ONE ELSE KNOWS.
UM...MY MIDDLE NAME IS BERTHA.
WELL, MINE'S FLORIAN.
HOW...PRINCELY. THAT'S ALMOST WORSE.
I MEAN, YOU KNOW, IT'S BETTER THAN BERTHA.
CLOSE YOUR EYES.
I HAVE SOMETHING TO SHOW YOU.

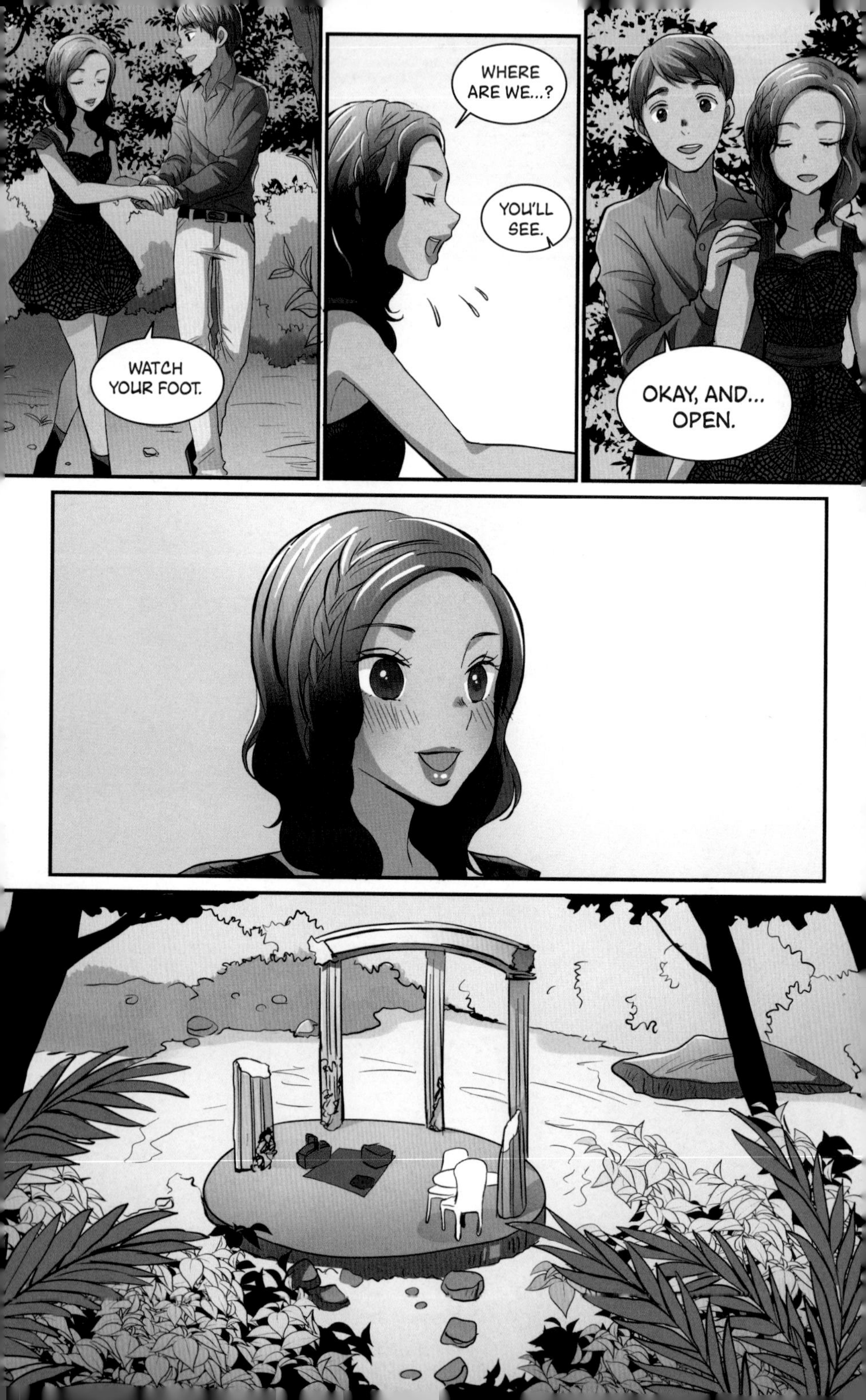
WATCH YOUR FOOT.
WHERE ARE WE...?
YOU'LL SEE.
OKAY, AND... OPEN.

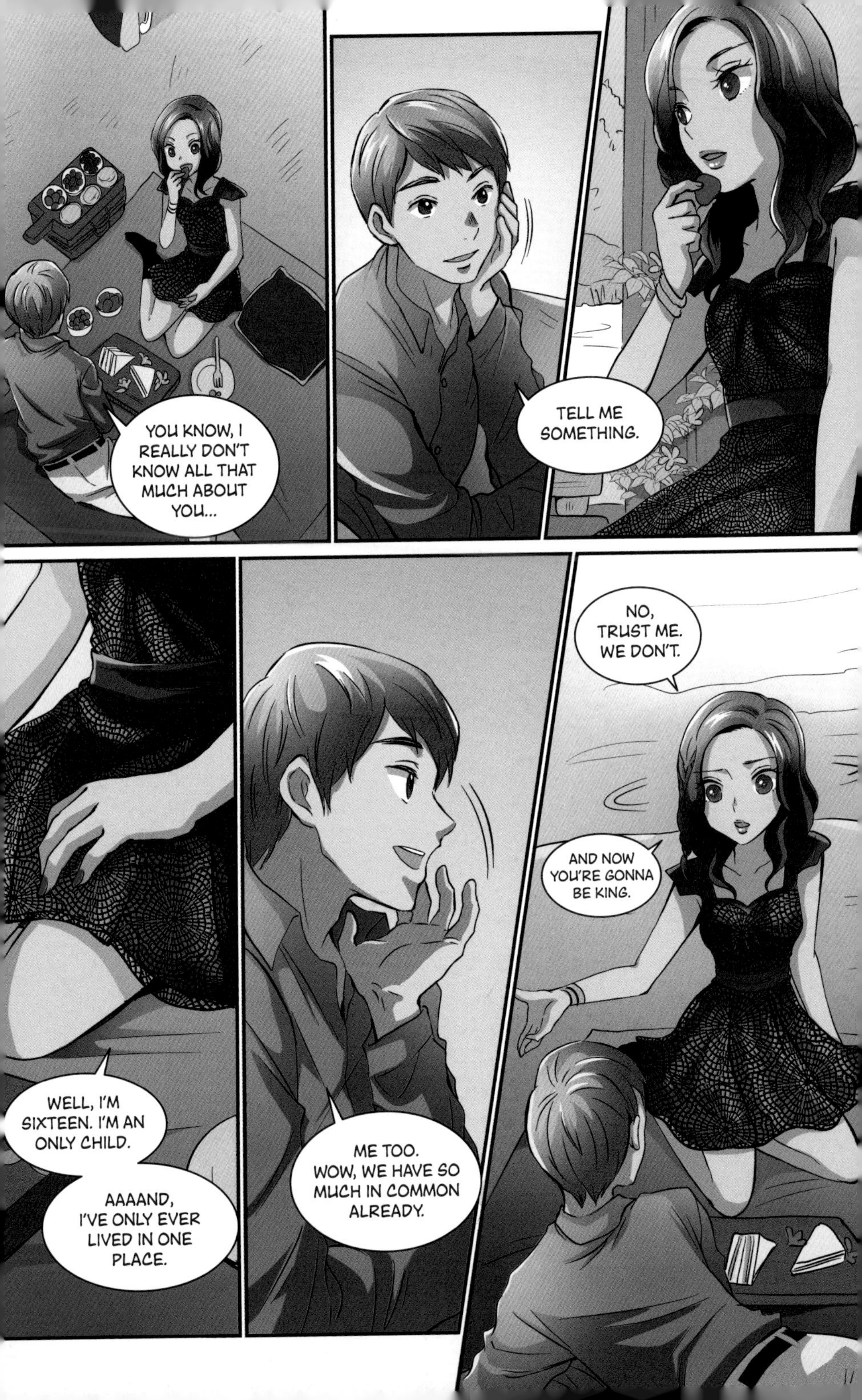
YOU KNOW, I REALLY DON'T KNOW ALL THAT MUCH ABOUT YOU...
TELL ME SOMETHING.
WELL, I'M SIXTEEN. I'M AN ONLY CHILD.
AAAAND, I'VE ONLY EVER LIVED IN ONE PLACE.
ME TOO. WOW, WE HAVE SO MUCH IN COMMON ALREADY.
NO, TRUST ME. WE DON'T.
AND NOW YOU'RE GONNA BE KING.

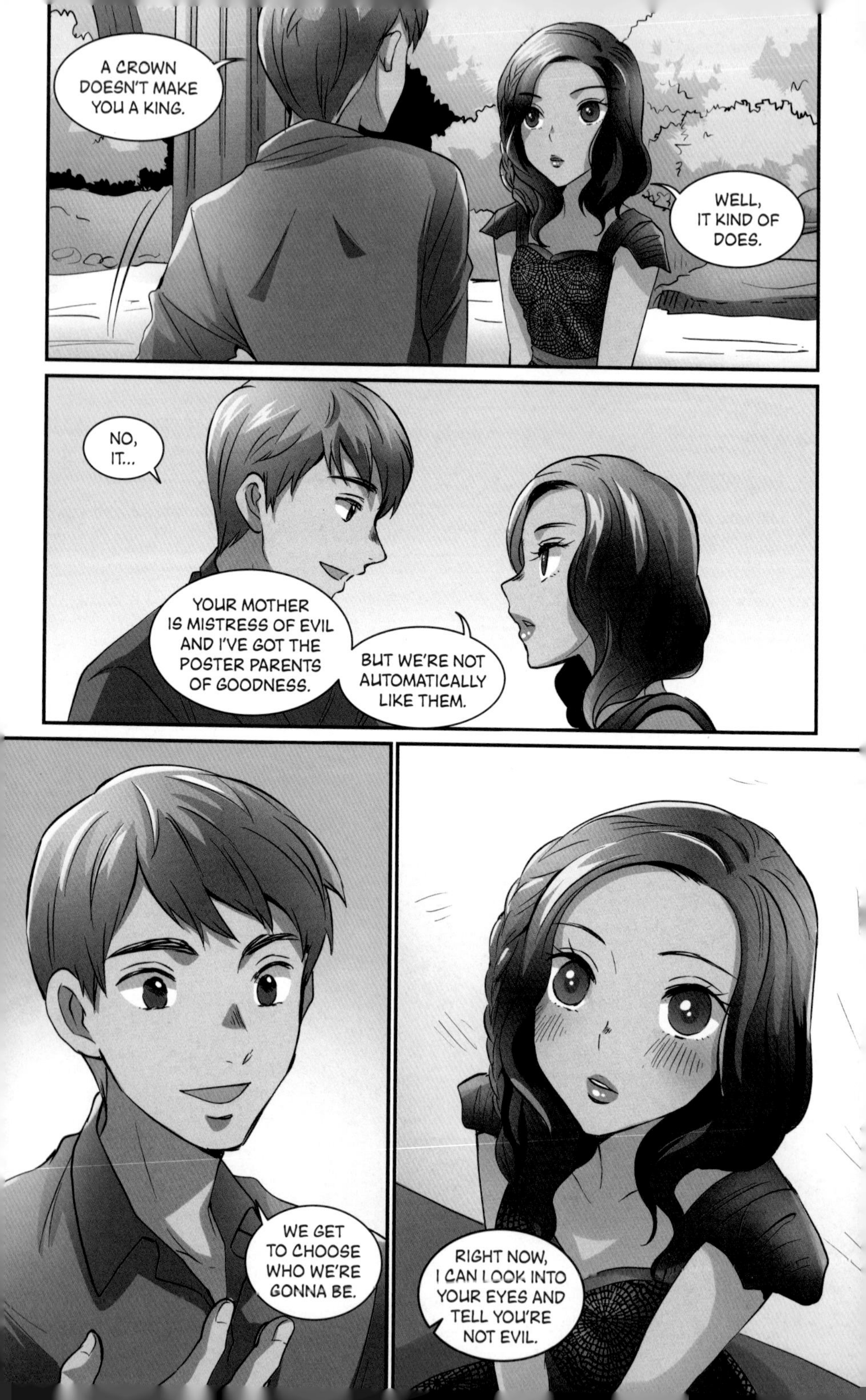
A CROWN DOESN'T MAKE YOU A KING.
WELL, IT KIND OF DOES.
NO, IT...
YOUR MOTHER IS MISTRESS OF EVIL AND I'VE GOT THE POSTER PARENTS OF GOODNESS.
BUT WE'RE NOT AUTOMATICALLY LIKE THEM.
WE GET TO CHOOSE WHO WE'RE GONNA BE.
RIGHT NOW, I CAN LOOK INTO YOUR EYES AND TELL YOU'RE NOT EVIL.

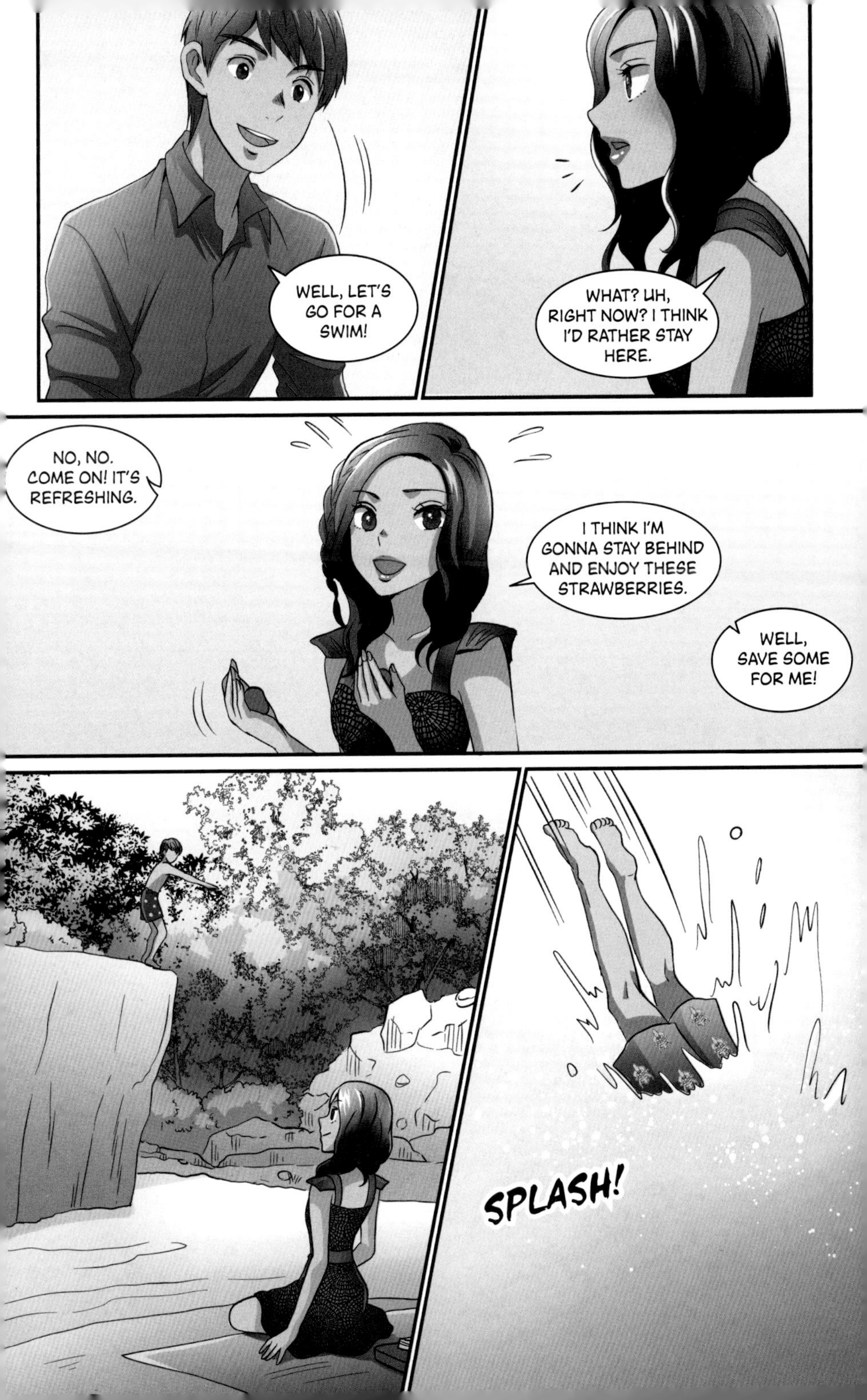
WELL, LET'S GO FOR A SWIM!
WHAT? UH, RIGHT NOW? I THINK I'D RATHER STAY HERE.
NO, NO. COME ON! IT'S REFRESHING.
I THINK I'M GONNA STAY BEHIND AND ENJOY THESE STRAWBERRIES.
WELL, SAVE SOME FOR ME!
SPLASH!

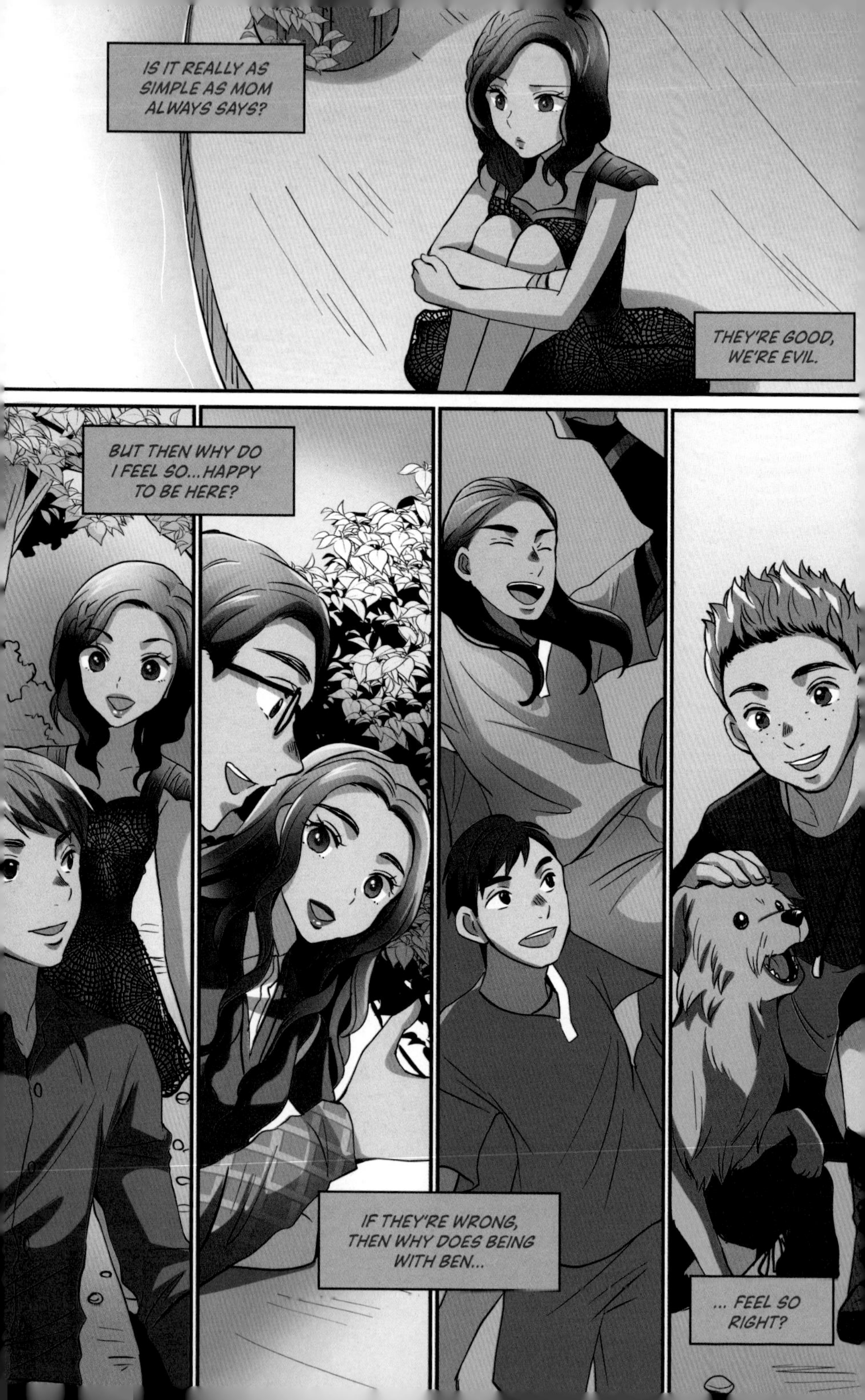
IS IT REALLY AS SIMPLE AS MOM ALWAYS SAYS?
THEY'RE GOOD, WE'RE EVIL.
BUT THEN WHY DO I FEEL SO...HAPPY TO BE HERE?
IF THEY'RE WRONG, THEN WHY DOES BEING WITH BEN...
... FEEL SO RIGHT?

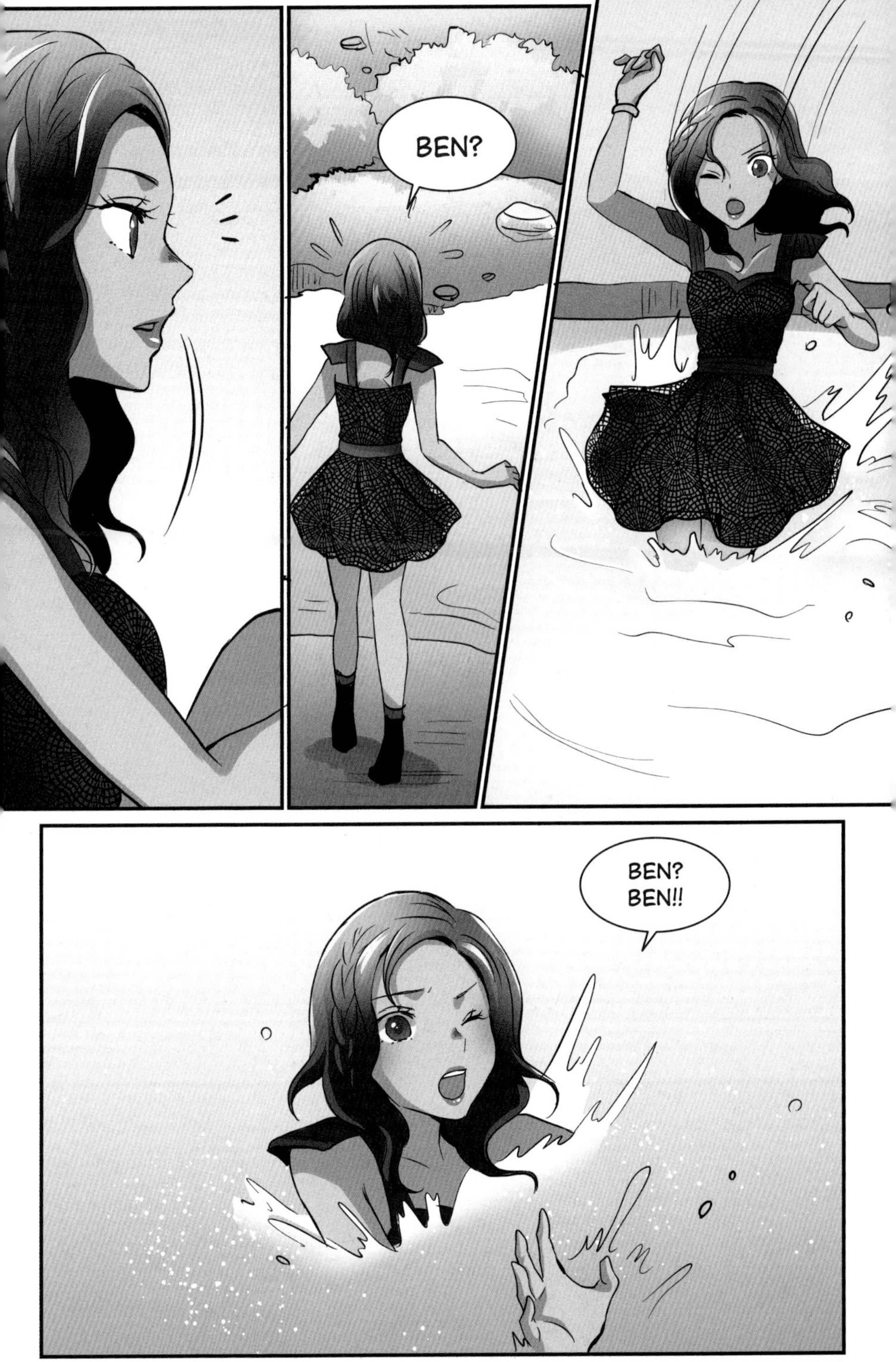
BEN?
BEN?
BEN!!

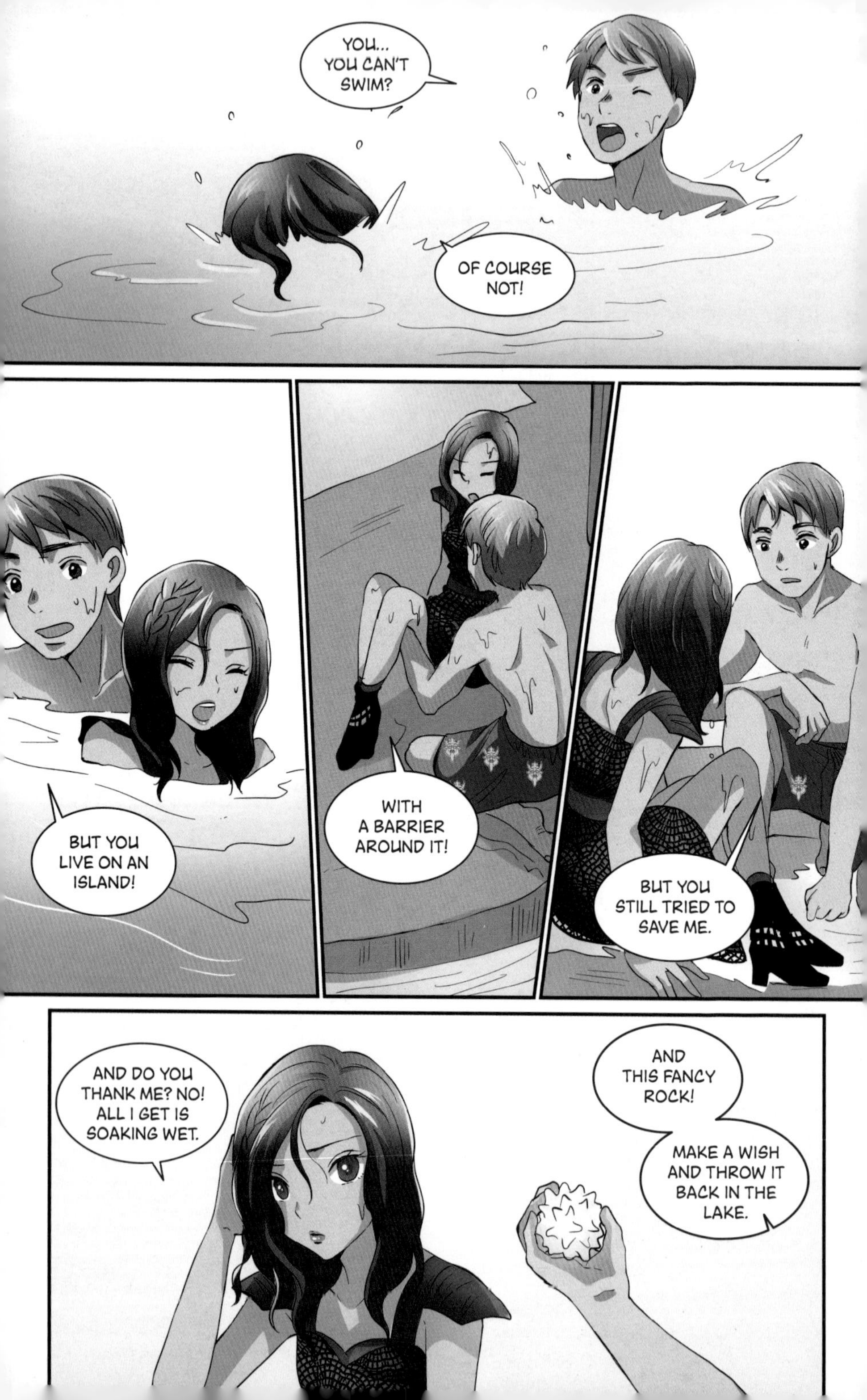
YOU... YOU CAN'T SWIM?
OF COURSE NOT!
BUT YOU LIVE ON AN ISLAND!
WITH A BARRIER AROUND IT!
BUT YOU STILL TRIED TO SAVE ME.
AND DO YOU THANK ME? NO! ALL I GET IS SOAKING WET.
AND THIS FANCY ROCK!
MAKE A WISH AND THROW IT BACK IN THE LAKE.

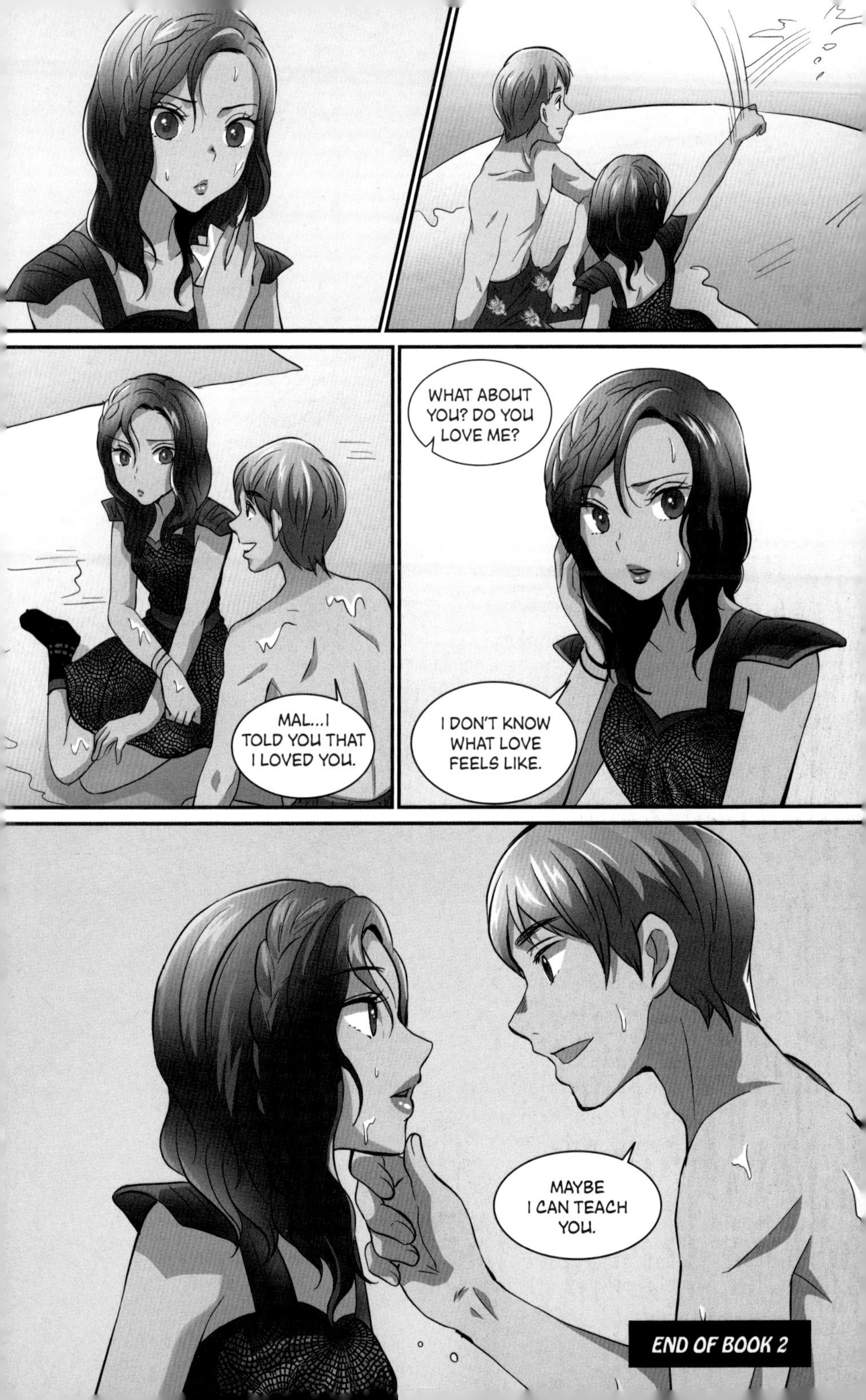

MAL...I TOLD YOU THAT I LOVED YOU.
WHAT ABOUT YOU? DO YOU LOVE ME?
I DON'T KNOW WHAT LOVE FEELS LIKE.
MAYBE I CAN TEACH YOU.
END OF BOOK 2

In the Final Volume of

DESCENDANTS

THE Rotten to the CORE TRILOGY

AVAILABLE DEC. 2017

COVER NOT FINAL

Parents' Day at Auradon Prep proves to be even more dreadful than expected for the VKs. Ostracized by their new friends and classmates, Mal, Evie, Jay, and Carlos are even more determined to fulfill their parents' evil plan, but doubt begins to creep into their thoughts. The people of Auradon think the VKs will always be evil, but in their hearts they are conflicted. Explore the last volume of *Disney Descendants: The Rotten to the Core* Trilogy as the VKs discover what it means to be true to themselves.